Louis Sanders studied English at the Sorbonne and lived for several years in Britain. *Death in the Dordogne* is his debut novel, and the first in a series set among the British community in the Dordogne. He now lives in the Dordogne with his English wife.

Death in the Dordogne

Louis Sanders

translated by Adriana Hunter

Funded by the Arts Council of England

This book is published with the participation of the French Ministry of Culture – Centre National du Livre

This book is supported by the French Ministry for Foreign Affairs, as part of the Burgess programme headed for the French Embassy in London by the Institut Français du Royaume-Uni.

First published in 1999 by Rivages/noir

First published in this English translation in 2002
by Serpent's Tail, 4 Blackstock Mews, London N4 2BT
website: www.serpentstail.com

Printed by Mackays of Chatham, plc

10 9 8 7 6 5 4 3 2 1

The dead man's mother was standing in the doorway, raising her great muscular arms to the heavens, wailing loudly and monotonously. Then she turned back to the body: a man in his thirties done up in his suit and tie, sturdily built like herself with wide shoulders and a bull neck; his beard had carried on growing a little and left a greyish shadow on his fleshy cheeks. From time to time the mother would pause before producing the next instalment of her mourner's cries, calling the queue of visitors in the corridor to witness her misfortune, as they waited their turn to see the body on his neatly-ironed linen sheets, his head resting on an embroidered pillow case. Bunches of roses had been laid on either side of the body, still wrapped in their cellophane paper and tied with shiny bows like boiled sweets.

One after another, the men and women who had made their way to the house came up to the great bulk of the mother whose impressive bosom heaved as she communicated imploringly with some unidentifiable god — despite the crucifix that had been hung above the bed. She had a few apt words for each of them, a kind thought from the dead man: 'Look at him, François, look at him, you won't see him over at La Berthonie any more, you won't have a laugh with him again, you know he loved coming to see you.'

And she gestured to the lifeless body — all in its Sunday best — that had been her son.

François, the Malebranches' son, had come with his own

ageing mother. He circled round the bed, leaning over the heavily made-up features and crying noisily with tears streaming down over his thin, deeply furrowed face. Then it was old mother Malebranche's turn, and she let out a medley of shrill yelps.

Their wails could be heard as far away as the kitchen where the family were waiting to shake hands with the visitors and to wag their heads to mean 'What can you say?'. The widow had her four-year-old son on her knee; they both seemed to be stupefied by the whole ceremony and, at least in the daughter-in-law's case, endured it with a niggling irritation which flitted across her face every time a neighbour whom she, anyway, hardly ever saw offered their condolences. Her brother offered his support by taking responsibility for saying a few words in reply to all these people, most of whom were not even friends, expressing their makeshift sympathy.

The grandmother sat crumpled on a stool: a pile of old black lace in the depths of a bric-à-brac shop, and, in the middle of all this fabric, her mummified face moved slowly but silently. From time to time she would slowly open her toothless mouth like an old frog, then she would close it again, chewing the air. It looked as if her lips wanted to suck up and eat the faces around them. Her bony hands were very probably crossed over her knees, although it was impossible to distinguish the different parts of her body except for her ankles clad in blue-grey woollen stockings spattered with dirt and still clinging to a stray piece of straw. Her tiny eyes were perfectly dry and they never stopped darting about the room as she watched the visitors and the members of her own clan gathered together in mourning. But it was hard to read the expression in her eyes: impatience, sorrow, hatred. Perhaps she felt nothing at all.

The father, standing shorter than his wife and sons, with his beret on his head and his hands in the pockets of his old blue trousers, didn't say a word.

When I came up the stairs, the dead man's mother looked

over towards me and I saw old mother Malebranche mutter a few words in her ear. Now that she knew who I was, the mother came over and embraced me, crying 'Oh, you lived in La Berthonie, he knew you better than me and now . . . look, look at my son.'

It was the first time I'd ever seen him.

A cow could be heard lowing somewhere in the distance and the deceased's mother turned back to old mother Malebranche and added, still crying, 'Listen, listen, can you hear it? They're his cows! They're waiting for him, they're looking for him!'

Then she buried her face in her hands and wept again, the whole of her huge body shaking as she sobbed.

Then I had to go into the room, look at the body and lower my head.

*

A little earlier in the day, old mother Malebranche had come and knocked on my door and explained to me that it would be seemly for me to go over to Le Bost with her and her son, because one of the Caminade sons had died and it was the local custom for all the neighbours to go and offer their condolences to the family. I'd tried to wriggle out of it, arguing that it might seem indiscreet of me, given that I wasn't from these parts, a foreigner and newly installed Englishman, that I didn't know the Caminades, etc. etc. There was, however, no getting out of it. With a pained expression, she just kept repeating: 'But you must, but you must, tch, but you must.' I ended up giving in, and I went to put on my most presentable jacket, which was rather too bright a green for the occasion. After lunch they came over to pick me up in their car to take to me to Le Bost, the tiny hamlet in which the Caminades lived and died. On the way they'd carried on a rather bright, cheerful conversation, bearing in mind the circumstances of the visit.

*

Once I got back down to the ground floor, having looked respectfully at the body of this stranger, I heard more crying — cries of anger this time — coming from the kitchen. Insults and protestations of innocence were being hurled around the room. When I came to the bottom of the stairs, I watched the scene surreptitiously and thought I could work out what was going on. A young man of about twenty-five had come to offer his condolences to the Caminades, but he had been refused entry because he was suspected of being the lover of their youngest daughter, Rose. This union did not meet with her family's approval because of some hackneyed old story of land that had been bought and sold on, a quarrel that had been more or less forgotten and which, anyway, went back a couple of generations, but which was still fresh enough in their minds for the enmity between the two families to be preserved. The young man had dressed up for the occasion, less out of respect to the deceased than to impress the girl and her family; he was wearing a black double-breasted suit with wide lapels and shoes that had been polished so energetically they could have served as mirrors. He had a square jaw and rather heavy features, he smelt of peppery aftershave and his hair was slicked back as if he were heading out to a nightclub in Thiviers. An argument had erupted between the dead man's older brother and the visitor: the former was explaining heatedly that he didn't want riff-raff like him — a good-for-nothing, practically a crook — in his house while his brother was lying dead upstairs but, if he'd still been alive, this brother wouldn't have thought twice about slinging a punch at such a . . . such a . . . then he'd fallen silent, unable to find an insult worthy of the contempt that he felt for this individual. The young man started to protest again, saying there was no reason for him to be treated like this; then even Rose, exasperated, got to her feet and told him that now wasn't the time to make a fuss. He left, throwing furious looks of loathing around him, shaking his head and muttering 'Well, if

they're going to be like that ...', as if to say the Caminades more
than deserved their misfortune.

★

The crying stopped for a moment and Madame Caminade
came downstairs to refresh herself with a glass of water. That was
when I heard her turn to old mother Malebranche, when they
were alone for a moment in a sort of back hall, and say perfectly
calmly: 'The young don't like this sort of thing, they'd like to do
it differently. My daughter-in-law, she doesn't like to see me
crying like this for my son. They want it all modern, but, you
know, we've always done it like this, us, haven't we?'

Old mother Malebranche replied with a 'Hm, well' and a
shrug of her thin, knotty shoulders.

A little later we all went back outside again, the
Malebranches and myself, stepping into the muddy farmyard
strewn with tools, roof tiles and planks of wood, none of which
would probably ever actually be used.

The Malebranches' tears had dried as quickly and easily as
they had started to flow when they went into the chamber of
death.

'Hey, look, they've moved the old tractor,' said the son, turning to his mother.

'Oh yes. Look over there, they've got lovely rabbits, haven't
they. Poor Gaston, tch. It's the devil's luck, tch.'

'Yup, it is.'

'Was your husband not able to come?' I asked Madame
Malebranche.

'No, no, he doesn't like that sort of thing and he feels giddy
the whole time. Tch, tch, it's the devil's bad luck, this giddiness.'

They offered to drive me home but, as Le Bost is only a few
kilometres from La Berthonie, I decided that, despite the cold
and the damp, I'd rather walk back over the hill along the mud
tracks through the woods.

There wasn't a sound except for the occasional cry of a bird. It was Saturday but no one was out shooting, perhaps out of respect for their neighbour. In these instances, you are neighbours even if you live several kilometres away from the house that's been struck by death.

At that time of year it is as oppressively wet in the Dordogne as it can be hot in July, but it keeps on raining until you think you will never see the sun again, that the cold season is the only one that really matters and that night will go on falling earlier and earlier every day. To make things worse, the images of the funeral vigil I'd just been to kept springing up in my mind.

A pile of chopped wood by the side of the road reminded me of the circumstances of Gaston's death. He'd gone to find a particular piece of wood in a part of the forest that belonged to his family. He needed a long, sturdy beam because he'd got it into his head that he was going to restore the roof of one of the barns and, as wood was expensive, he'd naturally decided to go and cut down one of his own oaks. The Caminades didn't speak much and he hadn't explained in detail his plan of action for the day. He'd left at dawn and still hadn't come home when night began to fall. Still nothing the following morning. They'd looked for him everywhere before calling the police. Eventually, he'd been found crushed under the oak tree, lifeless.

Rumours and speculation had begun to spread slowly at first in the hamlet, then in the nearby village and on into the towns of Thiviers and Nontron, in the cafés, because that's where gossip reaches a fever pitch on the subjects of sex and death. Shruggings of shoulders and raisings of eyebrows, grumblings and spreadings of hands had served as a eulogy for this peasant's son, a Communist and an atheist who hadn't wanted a priest and who'd asked specifically for 'no flowers or wreaths' at his funeral. The tittle-tattle, the doubts and the suspicions had been encouraged by the fact that this wasn't the first Caminade son to meet a violent death.

The eldest son, Louis, had disappeared ten or fifteen years earlier. He'd got drunk with a friend who'd driven him all the way to Angoulême, apparently for a party. A local peasant had seen them from his tractor as they got into a Renault 4, but he hadn't seen who was driving. Two days later, a bloated body found floating in its underpants on a lake near Nontron was identified as Louis. He was assumed to have left the party blind drunk, to have gone for a swim and to have drowned. Louis's friend was never found, neither was the Renault 4, and no one was even sure that they'd gone to Angoulême. After the news had been published in *Sud-Ouest*, that detail had somehow attached itself to the account — along with a number of others — in the commentaries inspired by *pastis*, *calvados* and white wine in various cafés or by *pineau* in the dark kitchens of people's homes all over the Dordogne.

I decided not to think about it; the cries of the biblical mourner keeping vigil over her son's body and the crushing gloominess of the cold and wet as the day drew to a precocious close were more than enough to fuel my imagination. I preferred to think back to the history books about the French peasantry in the eighteenth and nineteenth centuries that I had read at Cambridge a few years earlier and to the French novels that had prompted me to come and live in this part of the world.

The woodland path to La Berthonie comes out into a clearing on a slope and then carries on down towards another path which leads to a farm glorying in the name of Pisse-Chèvre — goat's piss. The local inhabitants pronounce it 'piche-chèvre'. I've always found that amusing. The house, which lies in the 'dell' — another expression used by the natives of La Berthonie — is particularly cold and dark. For the last thirty years it's been lived in by an elderly English alcoholic who breeds goats and has a terrible reputation amongst the locals, especially in the village. He's accused of all sorts of things, of erecting a barrier across the public footpath that passes in front of his house, of firing at some hunters stalking a stag, of setting fire to the fields in summer. On that occasion, the firemen had to be called out . . . what a saga. He sobered up at the police station before being sent home to his wife and daughter. This daughter was a woman of thirty something who never left the farmhouse in the dell. I'd never spoken to them myself, I'd seen them from a distance when out walking in the woods or on my runs when I was still playing rugby in Thiviers.

Just as I was thinking about this family — English like me and they'd found it very difficult settling here — I caught sight of her a few hundred metres away, on the slope in the middle of the clearing, the woman who was known locally as The Englishman from Pisse-Chèvre's Daughter. No one knew their name or, if they did, they never used it.

She was wearing a stained old Barbour and her golden-red hair was blowing in the wind. She couldn't possibly have seen me because she was staring straight ahead of her, standing perfectly still with her hands in her pockets, and I'd seen her in profile. After a few moments' hesitation, my first instinct was to call out to her, to wave and go over and exchange a few meaningless words which would have been quite normal if we'd both lived in a village in Sussex, but the rumours about them nevertheless created some sort of wall between this family and the outside world, as did their own silence, the voluntary imprisonment in which they lived. Something about the immobility of this tall, excessively thin figure standing in the middle of the clearing stopped me at the last minute. Then I heard a hoarse cry which was swallowed up in the trees, a cry of anger pronounced shyly, without assurance. She still hadn't moved, only her hair sketched some movement on her silhouette; then I followed her gaze and saw, a little further away, her father, a hairy, bearded old man in filthy coveralls, lurching about in a drunken stupor. Egged on by far from honourable curiosity, I moved several paces to one side, the better to watch the scene. The Englishman tripped, fell in the mud, swore as he picked himself up, then shook his fist towards a billy-goat that watched him from its enclosure with an air of mild astonishment. He threatened to kill the animal, to slit its throat, he hurled insults at it, probably without realising that his daughter was witnessing this behaviour. In his state he wouldn't have noticed me either, but it was unlikely that he would mind what the neighbours thought of him. A great pile of red plastic containers had been heaped up as high as the Malebranches' muck heap against the stone wall of the house. They had once been full of Bergerac at five francs a litre, a wine very popular with the local English community who bought it in the market in Thiviers or Brantôme. He headed unsteadily for these plastic containers, picked one up and threw it at the billy-goat, although he didn't manage to hit the animal. Then he slipped again and let out a reverberating 'Fuck!'

I was now by way of being trapped on the edge of the clearing, because I didn't want the daughter to know that a stranger had also watched the humiliating spectacle presented by her father. I thought of beating a retreat without really knowing where to go and was just turning to leave when I saw another silhouette to my left, a few hundred metres from the young woman, a little further up the slope. It was a elderly woman and she was only about fifty metres away from me. She must have been in her sixties, or perhaps a bit older judging by the curve of her back and her clothes, which, incidentally, were not the clothes of a peasant. Too clean, too well-kept, perhaps at a real stretch the sort of clothes you might wear for a country walk or for gardening, but not to work in the fields and the cowsheds. Her face was partly hidden, but I eventually recognised her or rather guessed who she must be. It was the old Dutchwoman who lived in the château a little way away from the hamlet, another of the characters who didn't get involved in the day-today life of La Berthonie, who hardly ever went out, was always alone and was sometimes glimpsed as she drove past along the track, but who never turned to nod even the briefest hello to the people she passed.

She must have set out for a walk and she too must have stopped in front of this double apparition of the drunken Englishman and his daughter now watching him silently from a distance. I think I was the only one of the quartet to have seen the absurd scene in its entirety, the succession of watchers being watched, each one immobilised by what was or was not going on before their eyes.

Suddenly, the young Englishwoman's voice rang out with unexpected authority in the middle of the clearing, screaming with controlled rage 'Stop it!'

Her father, who was lying flat out in the mud, half crawling, looked up at her with his mouth hanging open, it was almost comic. The old Dutchwoman turned on her heel and disappeared swiftly into the trees while the Englishwoman strode purposefully over the clearing to go and help her father, still admonishing him although I could no longer hear what she was saying. I watched them move away with a mixture of bafflement and compassion. It was beginning to get really cold.

2

The house creaks in every direction and the noises are amplified at night; the beams groan, sometimes the doors even slam shut by themselves and these sounds produced by inert matter create a music all their own. Added to the music of dead wood and stonemasonry are a host of moans and squeaks from invisible animals, little paws scratching at the floorboards in response to the more reassuring crackling of oak logs in the hearth and the tinkling as a bottle of whisky knocks against the rim of my glass at regular intervals. If I should ever leave the bottle on the table in the middle of the room, I contemplate with horror the few metres that lie between the fire and my favourite drink, a distance that I will have to travel in the nightmarish cold in order to pour myself another drink. There isn't any central heating: when I bought the house I still tended to confuse the downright uncomfortable with the picturesque. But what does that matter when I've got duty-free Glenfiddich — or, even better, Laphroaig — instead of calor gas. I buy wood from the Malebranches and I cut it here at home with a blunt axe, working up such a sweat that once I've finished the job I don't actually need or want to be warmed up — momentarily, anyway. The rain and the sunshine, the cold and the heat are highly prized topics of conversation in England, as indeed they are in all the other countries that I've visited however briefly, but in the little English community in the Dordogne to which I now belong, the variations in temperature have become an obsession, the struggle against the rigours of winter keeps each of us busy for at least two hours a day. You have to empty the ash from the wood-burner, fetch the logs, chop them, split them, stack them, collect packing cases that have been used to transport fruit (always from hot countries, mind you) from outside super-markets and remind yourself not to throw away old newspapers. It's a life dominated by wood: thick, dense wood, wood which is to the Dordogne as the dollar is to Wall Street and which eventually killed the son of that bulky woman whose wails keep coming back to me like the shadowy memory of a bad dream while I sit in my leather armchair, turning the whisky round in my cheap peasant's glass. It's late but I daren't go up to bed, I haven't lit the stove and I don't want to get undressed. I can't even face taking my socks off, the cold is too biting, too raw, too looming, like a punishment that you have to endure without knowing why. I can't concentrate on my book either, I'm try-ing to imagine the noise that the enormous oak tree would have made as it crushed young Gaston's body. Did he die instantly? He probably went into a coma. I don't really know, I don't know anything about things medical. Did he call for help for hours, alone in the middle of the forest? Was he really alone? According to the gossip, the chain broke on his chain-saw, he turned round and at that moment the tree fell. An accident. Rather an improbable accident. I don't know whether there was an autopsy and I'm annoyed with myself for going over and over these details which haven't got anything to do with me, almost as if I wanted to believe that he'd been killed to alleviate — if only momentarily — the boredom that hangs over these Dordogne winter evenings. But the story really did seem impossible. It wasn't the first time he'd cut down a tree. He would have been more careful. Someone must have been with him, the same man who took Louis to the party in Angoulême or wherever it was, the man with the Renault 4? Was the murderer amongst the people who came to offer their condolences? That young idiot, for example, the one with his slicked-back hair who caused such a scene at the door?

I'm now regretting that I didn't light the stove and, as a consolation, I pour myself some more whisky, so generously in fact that I'm tempted to say thank you to myself. I look at the room, at the other leather armchair opposite me, which is unfortunately empty and which would do well to accommodate, for example, one of my old university friends, one of the ones featured in the photograph of the Trinity Rugby Fifteen which hangs on the wall. I'm second from the left in the first row. Next to it there's a rather boring print, a landscape in the Lake District, a Christmas present from I can't remember who. And then a few of my own artistic endeavours, a nude, some flowers, an equally boring landscape, but of the Dordogne this time, because I paint as a hobby, like Winston Churchill, and I've actually got a book on the subject by the great man himself, it's called *Painting as a Pastime*. On the other side there's a framed reproduction of a pre-Raphaelite beauty who makes me think that, when all's said and done, rather than having an old university friend in my second, empty leather chair, I'd like to have a superb creature with flowing red hair, snuggled into, for example, a hand-knitted cardigan, in green because green goes well with redheads, and a long, full skirt. She would sit there drinking her port and talking to me about everything and nothing. That's when I realise that my glass is as empty as the other chair. I remedy this situation with no further delay and then start thinking about the Englishman from Pisse-Chèvre's Daughter and her father wallowing in the mud. The thought of any kind of emotional attachment with this young woman who lives in such total isolation is more than a little terrifying, but there isn't much choice on offer in La Berthonie. But then again, no. I can't help smiling as I imagine a scenario in which I ask her to marry me and I introduce my parents to my future father-in-

law in the state and the place in which he found himself a few
hours ago.

I can hear rats in the attic because the noise carries through
more than one floor, hurried little footsteps as if they were trying to escape from a predator. And, as if to confirm this idea, an
owl hoots in the distance.

At last I make up my mind to go upstairs. I put out the light,
and the glowing red embers create a dance on the walls between
the disproportionate shadows of the knick-knacks that are
accumulating on my Victorian pine furniture . . . a monk's head
cast in plaster, Catholic and exotic, found in a second-hand shop
where I was assured that it was a seventeenth-century Jansenist
artefact, which I didn't believe; a vintage coffee-grinder; a
bouquet of dried flowers; a few broken toys, including a
London double-decker bus. I don't even notice what the bedroom looks like any more, it's a good size, and it too has a
massive sixteenth-century fireplace and a stone lintel with a
carved escutcheon. The walls are covered in greyish plaster and
decorated with hand-painted naive designs which run all the
way round the room. It has a very high ceiling with rows of
chestnut-wood beams, blackened by the smoke of innumerable
fires that have burned there over the centuries to warm up the
penniless minor nobility, most of whom were forced to enlist in
the army.

These houses were then usually bought up by peasant farm-
ers and carved up in their wills. That's why I only own half of
the building in which I live, which once would have accommodated up to three families. They blocked up doorways, built
partitions and lived like that, on top of each other. At the beginning of the twentieth century La Berthonie, which now has just
eight permanent residents and two second homes that are hardly
ever occupied, had a population of about two hundred. It's
difficult to imagine now that the village has shrunk so much.
Children slept in their parents' or their grandparents' bedrooms,

people lived in the kitchen which acted as a common room or at least more of a common room than the others, women gave birth in every available corner and people probably made love in the dark but with someone else — who could hear everything — in the room. At least, as far as I'm concerned, that's not a problem that's going to present itself this evening.

The other part of the house, the bit that doesn't belong to me, was inherited by a man who disappeared after his mother died. I've heard that, after the reading of the will in the *notaire*'s office in Nontron, he came back to La Berthonie and confided in Malebranche's mother, who has since died, saying that his sisters were obviously the favourites in his family and that his inheritance was worthless compared to what they'd been left. He then had his part of the house restored, so that it could withstand the passage of time and the ravages of the weather, with — quite naturally — hideous results: lots of that rough grey plaster you can never take off again, a roof of machine-made tiles and metal shutters. Then he left. For a long time his sisters and their husbands tried to get hold of him, at one point a telephone number in his name was found at an address on the outskirts of Paris, several even, because there was no shortage of Jacques Durocs. They called all the numbers and all except one answered to say they had never heard of a house or half a house in the Dordogne which belonged to them. At the remaining one, there was no reply. They'd tried ringing at all hours of day and night. Nothing. No success. They concluded that that must be the right number, as if this man now only existed in absent, invisible, inaudible and inaccessible form. Then one day they heard a disembodied voice saying that the number dialled had not been recognised, the line had been cut off. This was the ultimate proof that the telephone that had rung so frequently and which now lay silent had been Jacques Duroc's. On the other hand, they didn't know why he was no longer there. Was Jacques dead? In prison? They discovered relatively quickly that that wasn't the case because Jacques went on paying the necessary taxes on his empty house in La Berthonie. The man who sold me my half of the house had a theory on the subject: Jacques had become a homosexual, he who'd been such a good boy, such a dutiful son and — crippled with shame — he daren't show his face again. My reaction to this speculation was restricted to scratching my throat.

I took some interest in this mystery myself, because I thought I might like to buy the other half of the building. In England a semi-detached house somehow symbolises something vaguely mediocre and conventional, so I was not indifferent to the irony of fate which meant that, even in the depths of the French countryside, I'd ended up in a situation reminiscent of the suburbs of London. Obviously, I didn't have any more success in my rather half-hearted research than the Duroc sisters had had in theirs. Coming as I did from London, I'd briefly toyed with the idea of squatting in the other half. I could, for example, have found one of the walled-up doorways under the plaster and opened it up, but out in the country property is sacred and I was worried that this sort of problem might be settled with buckshot. That's why the grey plaster stopped along the exact line which marked my half of the house and my half was still in stone. Here, you can carve up a house just like carving up a field. A roofed gallery runs all the way along the south-facing side of the house and sometimes in the summer I go and sit out on this wide balcony in a sagging old armchair that I haven't bothered to have re-covered.

But it isn't summer, and the temperature in the bedroom is what you might expect in the cabin of a boat trawling for cod off the coast of Newfoundland. So I take off my shoes but not my socks, I remove my tweed jacket, but I keep on my Irish jumper and my corduroy trousers and, still dressed, I slide under the duvet and sink into a whisky-scented sleep to dream of widows, weeping mothers, crushed woodcutters, Englishmen in the mud and young women humiliated by the sight of their fathers who are even more drunk than I am.

★

There was no one in the Malebranches' farmyard, no one but the chickens, the ducks, the geese and the dogs, two rather fat mongrels who yapped annoyingly as I made my way to the door of the house, a seventeenth-century manor surrounded by a thick gravy of mud. The lintel above each window was different, carved with flowers, hearts or seashells. An old up-ended stone chimney acted as a bench by the door and the door itself, which had never been painted or varnished, still boasted its impressive original lock. Old mother Malebranche always wore the eight-inch, brown metal key with its complicated curl of locking teeth, in her belt. I'd been to their house many times, but I'd never gone further than the huge kitchen which culminated in a magnificent fireplace that they'd modernised by having bricks painted in on either side of the hearth. An enormous cast-iron trammel and two fire-dogs occupied the centre of the hearth where small logs arranged in a fan shape burned from morning till night and on this fire old mother Malebranche cooked her meals in cast-iron pans. Under the floorboards there was still the old *pisé* floor, made of cut, flattened pebbles pushed into the beaten earth, forming patterns in blocks of different colour. The room was dominated by a huge crucifix hanging over the fireplace and behind the Saviour's back was a branch of laurel which never left him. At one time the shotguns must have been kept there because here and there on the crucifix you could still see parts of the rack. Oddly enough, a washing-machine held pride of place next to the sink, testimony to Madame Malebranche's dominant position in the bosom of her family, because, despite what it had cost them, she'd managed to persuade her husband and her son to take on this contraption which belonged to the modern world and alleviated some of her work. On the sideboard, which was mostly sixteenth-century but also owed something to the 1940s, there was a photograph of her daughter on her wedding day with her depressive groom. They'd gone to set up home together on the outskirts of Paris, to work in a factory and to end up on the dole, living in a house over which aeroplanes flew regularly and excruciatingly loudly on their way to and from Roissy-Charles-de-Gaulle.

The washing-machine was not the only proof of old Mother Malebranche's strength of character and importance in this house. On that day something exceptional was going on, a huge plank of wood had been put onto two trestles and was covered in blood and flesh. About twenty plucked, gutted and jointed ducks lay on it. Forty dark red *magrets* were lined up along the plank, the meat lying comfortably on cushions of scalloped yellow fat. At one end I saw a pile of heads and feet dripping with blood. She'd collected all the blood in a yellow plastic bowl and would sell the feathers for eiderdowns, even if there wasn't the market for them that there used to be.

'Come in, come in, Mr . . . Mr . . .'

She had, as usual, forgotten my name, it was too foreign and too complicated for her memory which only registered facts and words contained within the limits of her native *département*.

Christmas was coming, a woeful time of year for feathered creatures, who have to participate, at great personal cost, in the festivities and the annual explosion of gastronomic piety. I'd seen her force-feeding the ducks a few weeks earlier and I felt a perverse pleasure in describing the scene to the vegetarian English painters I knew. It was in a dark little shed at the far end of the yard. She went in and switched on the light and a dozen or so miserable creatures went and cowered in a corner, huddled together and staring at her in pure terror.

'Ah, poor things!' she said as she put down her pail full of maize steeped in oil to help it slide down their long necks. 'Can you hear them whistling? It's because they're already so fat. It's the fat round their hearts that does that. It's like when people get too fat, they get short of breath, tch,' she added, thin as a rake herself.

Then, with her little hat still on her head, she arched her back towards them and grabbed one under the beak, while the others scattered, flapping their wings and quacking in panic. She sat on the animal and stretched up its neck, then she put a few grains in a sort of funnel which had been equipped with the crank of an old coffee-grinder. Then, at last, she turned the handle, still saying 'Ah, poor thing!' all the while.

A little earlier in the year, when I'd been chatting to her next to the duck pond, she'd pointed out a clutch of adorable little balls of yellow fluff waggling along as they followed the mother duck and she'd asked me: 'Mr . . . um . . . Mr . . . Do you like *foie gras?*'

Those were the same animals that she force-fed before my eyes later in the year. They seemed to have aged.

Her husband came in, walking slowly and dragging his slippers along the floorboards. He'd stopped at the door to take off the green plastic clogs bought in a local hypermarket. He nodded without properly recognising me, once again, but guessing that it was me, because he was practically blind even though he still drove his ancient tractor and climbed up onto the roofs when they needed repairing. He came over and, by way of a handshake, offered me three arthritic fingers which I was to touch without holding them too firmly to avoid hurting him. I was asked whether I'd like anything to drink and, in the course of the weeks and months that I'd spent in La Berthonie, I'd come to understand that this proposition was more closely related to an order. I reluctantly accepted a glass of their sickly sweet, home-made white *pineau*. In days gone by, in order to avoid having to drink alcohol at ten o'clock in the morning or nine o'clock, not to mention eight o'clock, I used to ask for coffee. That was when they'd bring out 'just a drop' of *marc* or plum brandy at seventy or eighty degrees proof, to pour into my cup. It used to make me feel as if I were floating for the whole rest of the day.

Old man Malebranche sat down by the fireplace in a sprung garden chair, equipped with a complicated mechanism for raising and lowering the backrest for the user's comfort and convenience. The cushions were torn and saggy and the foam, which had gone brown with age and the effects of the smoke, spewed out like old pairs of tights from amongst the great petals of the green and orange flowers which suggested to me that this piece of furniture — probably far more authentic than anything available in the bric-à-brac shops — had been bought in a hypermarket in the early 1970s.

'So, how's your head, then?' I asked.

'Oh, still spinning, still spinning,' he repeated tirelessly like Galileo after his trial.

And his wife added 'It's the very devil, tch.'

I succumbed to the ritual commentary on the weather before coming to the point and asking the question that had brought me there that morning.

'Do you ever see the Englishman from Pisse-Chèvre?'

'Not very often. He doesn't have much to do with other people. He stays there in the dell. It can't be much fun.'

'He goes to Thiviers, to the market sometimes, we see him go past in his car. But you're probably asleep at that sort of time, it's always very early,' she said with a mildly ironic smile.

It was true. I'd heard it said that in the summer, for example, the Englishman from Pisse-Chèvre went through La Berthonie at breakneck speed in his Range Rover, without saying hello to anyone and without bothering about the children who might be playing in the road. And that was on top of his other crimes. They said, for example, that he didn't always pay his taxes, that he was actually rich and lazy to boot. Even if a lazy rich man probably wouldn't have chosen that shack of a house to harbour his debaucheries.

'But he's a good man,' commented old man Malebranche.

Thinking I must have misheard, I asked 'The Englishmen from Pisse-Chèvre?'

'He's a very good man,' he repeated.

I sat there open-mouthed on my wooden bench, with my back bolt upright and my fists resting on the waxed cloth on the table. I'd obviously believed everything I'd been told, not without embarrassment, mind you, because, being English myself, I'd felt compelled to feel and to declare out loud that people like that who don't live like everyone else and who upset a perfectly peaceful community or cause I don't know what other sorts of problems should be put in prison, for example, or banned from the country. Especially as when people told me about the excesses of this Englishman from Pisse-Chèvre, it wasn't difficult to imagine that they extended the judgement they passed on him onto all his compatriots and that they used all this tittle-tattle as an indirect way of making me understand that there were too many English people in the region and that the English didn't know how to behave.

Right then, I could have kissed old man Malebranche. I repeated what had been reported to me, but he just shrugged his shoulders and spoke to me as if I were a four-year-old: 'You mustn't believe everything you hear.'

'Do you ever go over to his house?'

'Oh, no, we're far too busy and so's he with his goats. But he really works, that man. He's a good sort. He bought a billy-goat from us once, I think. Because his had died.'

'Yes, that's right. He had all sorts of problems one year.'

'I've heard that he never says hello to anyone.'

'He's deaf, poor man. Can't hear a thing. When someone talks to him he puts his hands behind his ears like this and you have to shout,' explained old mother Malebranche.

Old man Malebranche started to laugh as he added 'Oh, you have to shout all right! I tell you what, I'll have a drop with you.'

'What about your head?'

'Oh, a drink's not going to make much difference.'

And old mother Malebranche poured it for him, muttering to herself. I suspected that the old boy had made use of the fact that I was there to ask for a drink, knowing full well that his wife wouldn't dare to reprimand him openly or to refuse him a drink in front of a foreigner.

'What about his wife?'

'Oh, we never see her. She never goes out.'

'Apparently, she was once a piano teacher.'

'What, round here?'

'No, in England.'

'Really? Who told you that?'

'Oh, I can't remember.'

'What about their daughter?'

'We don't see her either, but she walks about the countryside quite a bit. I don't even know if she can speak French, but she always says hello very politely when we come across her, doesn't she?'

'Oh, that she does. Yes, they're good people.'

★

As I went home, I reminded myself that the kindly tolerance which the Malebranches felt towards the recluses of Pisse-Chèvre was perhaps not as surprising as all that, because they too had their detractors in the area. Except, of course, that they were at least from the area, which gave them some sort of right to be on bad terms with the rest of the population while still living there.

In amongst the accumulation of grudges that people bore the Malebranches, only ever by insinuation, mind you, was the constantly recurring theme of how thin they were. They were indeed thin and this lack of substance that anybody fat might have given them went hand in hand with impressive physical strength, further endorsed by a number of scars which bore testimony to terrible pains they'd endured without complaint. But here, not far from the capital of *foie gras*, in the land of the *magret de canard* and the kingdom of *cassoulet*, this leanness was perceived as a sign of a disturbing austerity which unsettled entire villages of men and women, all of whom could boast a paunch. So people would say that they did things the old-fashioned way, by which they meant that they were mentally retarded. Being thin was also seen as a reflection of miserliness. The Parisians who had holiday homes in the village and who'd been brought up in the belief that everything can be broken, everything can be lost and everything can be thrown away, were also made to feel pretty uncomfortable on Wednesday evenings, dustbin day, when they carried out half a dozen bin bags full of endless rubbish, to see that the Malebranches had no household waste at all. They produced everything they ate themselves, the meat, the vegetables, even the wine (filthy plonk that probably wasn't more than seven degrees proof, but, when the need arose, made excellent vinegar) and the only things they bought in the shops were oil, salt and sugar. Everything else was recycled and re-used, nothing was thrown out. People concluded that this must have made them fabulously rich, that they could probably afford to travel a hundred times round the world in a first-class liner, but they stayed there, carrying on with the same chores, every day, every week, every season. They were also said to be miserly because they would rather have been hanged than sell the tiniest parcel of land which was of no use to them but might, for example, have made a nice garden for a neighbour. This useless land was more dear to them than their own skins. Yes, to them everything mattered and had its place and it was by counting the days and the seasons like this over the years that they had ended up owning this manor house. They had started off in one of the lesser cottages on the edge of the hamlet, a cottage which was now falling into ruin, still with all its furniture in it, because the affection that the Malebranches felt for it didn't necessarily oblige them to keep it maintained, thanks to their exotic logic which owed nothing to contemporary thinking.

3

In the Dordogne, but particularly in La Berthonie, the horizon
is never far away and yet everything is always miles from everything else, which is how the region preserves its charm and
which is also how it can become a prison in winter if you don't
have any cows to milk, any pigs to fatten or any chickens to
slaughter. So the English who live in the Dordogne meet up in
their informal clubs to do all sorts of things, but, more often
than not, nothing in particular, while — as soon as six o'clock
has struck — they quaff great quantities of all sorts of things
alcoholic.

I was heading for just one of these little get-togethers
at a local café when I left the Malebranches. I'd met Sue
Brimmington-Smythe at an exhibition organised by the *mairie*
in Nontron one spring and she'd told me that she ran a school
of painting some way away at Saint Jory de Chalais. After putting a fair few drinks back together, we'd become friends and
she'd asked whether I'd like to take part in the drawing classes
without paying the prohibitive fees she normally extracted. It
took me at least an hour, sometimes more, to get to Saint Jory
on my *mobylette*. We weren't the first English people to have
alighted in this corner of the globe; before us Buckmaster had
chosen to run the Resistance network that he'd set up from
Saint Jory. There was a plaque to that effect on the rival (but
nevertheless friendly) café. Sue Brimmington-Smythe was
standing out on the steps waiting for some friends and smiling

rather as one would expect a great socialite to, in Bedford Square in the 1930s, for example. From the pub-like noises escaping from inside this rural café, I could hear that I wasn't the first to arrive. Thompson was already there, a painter who'd once taught at the Slade School of Art in London, who refused to tell us his age — estimated to be about fifty-two — and who, it was said, had a mysterious past. He painted a variety of subjects of pre-Raphaelite inspiration with, here and there, the odd copy of a painting by Piero della Francesca. More often than not he actually did the teaching in Sue's school of painting or at least it was he who paced slowly up and down the rows of chairs and easels, in his trousers with holes in the knees, his Marks & Spencer jumper flecked with countless dabs of paint which he avoided washing at all costs and his shirt which had long since lost its collar; and every now and then he would point at one of the 'student's' drawings and shake his head despairingly. It was a handsome head, mind you, with very red cheeks which owed their apparent vitality to a mixture of fresh air and scarlet wine, generally sold in plastic bottles and bearing names like *Le Cellier du Baron* written in Gothic script. A girl called Marianne was also there; everyone thought that she was living with Thompson, but they actually hated each other although they didn't let it show and always greeted each other with extreme courtesy. James Bartlefoot was from humble origins in Yorkshire, from mining stock, he used to say, but he was probably exaggerating and — just to be provocative — he would growl at people as he said it. It turned out that Bartlefoot was the son of a schoolteacher and an accountant who had indeed worked for the director of a coal mine, but his relationship with coal ended there. He himself had been sent to a private school in the Midlands and tried his hardest to make his accent sound working class. He never missed an opportunity to give me a hard time because I'd been to Trinity, Cambridge; and he imagined that I must be of aristocratic extraction or at least he pretended that that was what he thought, calling me a spoilt child. He had not gone into higher education: according to him, he'd set off across the world, what he'd actually done was to go to Birmingham, Bristol, Islington and, finally, the Dordogne. He often felt equipped to teach us the ways of 'the world' because he'd been living meagrely enough for the last couple of years and got drunk every evening, knocking back significant amounts of whatever came to hand.

Patricia, the model who was to pose nude for us, had arrived in Johnny's Mercedes, a vehicle somewhere between a car and a gypsy caravan. It had originally been metallic grey, but had long since been covered in white striations where it had sidled a little too close to the walls of the barn that served as its garage. Johnny lived with some German musicians, millionaire hippies who grew their own marijuana over an extensive acreage around the fortified farm in which they lived. They supported Johnny, but, to show willing and to bring a bit of money into the community, he went to the market in Thiviers on Friday mornings to sell off his father's extensive collection of books which he'd had sent over to France after the latter's demise. First editions, offered at derisory prices, were carefully lined up in wooden crates and were of no interest to anyone except for Johnny's friends and even they decided that, at the end of the day, they'd rather buy wine from the neighbouring stall than spend their money on books they'd already read. These same books had brought to his attention the fact that an indeterminate number of mice had taken up residence in the boot of his Mercedes, because several volumes had been nibbled by teeth that could on no account have been either Johnny's or those of his friends or of his occasional mistresses. Johnny's full name was Charles Arbuthnott Lindsay Gascoyne, but by a miracle of contraction he'd managed to get people to call him Johnny.

Patricia, who'd once run a hairdressers in Blackpool, offered up her generous form to the inspection of these amateur artists and they in turn tried their best to reproduce it in brush-strokes on large sheets of paper, without losing the train of their conversation. As she was a dab hand with a pair of scissors, she quite often earned extra money by cutting the hair of whichever of the painters asked for these services, once she'd put her clothes back on and before making her way to the bar to reward her patience with white wine.

Sue Brimmington-Smythe hadn't joined us because she was preparing the dinner for later that evening in the restaurant; it was to be a strictly private meal for some twenty people, each with a guest. An Irish band had been brought in to play for us once we'd been well fed and watered and had pushed the tables back along the walls. The man on the violin was amazing, he could have been featured in an advertising campaign for Guinness with his red beard, his long thin face, his faded grey eyes and his tweed cap. It was only much later that I discovered he'd been born on the outskirts of Paris and dedicated himself to Irish music and IRA songs as others might turn to Buddhism or become vegetarians.

The silence that descended as we concentrated on our drawing was occasionally interrupted by a 'Could I borrow your rubber?' or 'I've never been able to do feet', and the naked vestal next to the gas heater in the middle of the room who'd taken up a pose as, for example, a heroic Athenian warrior, would take the opportunity to scratch her bosom.

At about five o'clock I decided that I'd had my fill of buttocks, breasts, shadows and plays of light and I left the little room that we used at the back of the restaurant, crossed the main dining area and arrived at the bar where Sue was chatting to a French girl of about twenty-five, wearing a navy blue jumper and a knee-length grey skirt; her hair was held back by a black velvet Alice band and she wore perfectly flat shoes. Despite her Catholic preferences in respect of clothing,

she smiled at me almost provocatively and I responded with
a nod of the head. She had blue-grey eyes, regular features
and an expression that was more amused than seductive.
Notwithstanding the way she was dressed, I decided it wouldn't
be a bad policy do a bit of export anthropology and to play
the English card for all it was worth. I therefore made a special
effort to pronounce my r's like w's and to be polite to the point
of gaucherie, as if I were a sort of incarnation of a tweed jacket
(and what's more, I had the good taste to be wearing one at
the time). I was not ignorant of the fact that the French bour-
geoisie were highly susceptible to *le chic anglais*, especially
over towards Bordeaux or La Rochelle, for example . . . not
that far from where we were. Sue watched me with a sneaky
smile because she could obviously tell that I was laying it on a
bit thick, but I decided not to let that bother me and I made
sure that I mentioned Cambridge within the first five sentences
of my conversation with this girl. She continued to look
amused, of course, but her smile was becoming increasingly
provocative. Alma Mater. I touched on the subject of cricket,
even though my career in this field was limited to the blow I'd
given myself on the head with a bat on a freezing Norfolk
beach.

Sue introduced us to each other. Her name was Martine,
which seemed like stating the obvious.

'Do you live in the area?'

'A little way away, towards Villars, near the Château de
Puyghilhem. Do you know it?'

'Very well.'

This was unhoped for, a topic of conversation that was at
once banal and familiar to us both.

'Did you know that a man's just died there?' I asked. But I
immediately bit my bottom lip and cursed myself, wondering
what on earth had persuaded me to choose a subject like that. I
didn't wonder for long though because I knew nothing, not

even the naked cut–and–blow–drier, managed to take my mind off that peasant crushed under an oak tree in circumstances which struck me as dubious to say the least. She must have thought I was rather morbid or even a psychopath. She looked down and scrutinised her flat loafers for a moment before replying 'Yes, I had heard.'

I sensed straight away that I shouldn't let our conversation flag for a moment, especially as I could see, on the other side of the bar, that Sue was no longer smiling but looking at me in consternation.

'Would you like something to drink?' I asked.

She still had half a glass of white wine.

'I'm fine, thanks.'

I took this opportunity to turn towards Sue and I thought about ordering a pint of beer but, afraid that Martine might find this too proletarian, I asked for a whisky, a single malt, much more aristocratic. And, as if by a miracle, she then added 'Yes, of course I've heard about it, because I know that area very well. It's where my family comes from.'

'So you must know La Berthonie. That's where I live.'

'Yes, very well. Which house've you taken?'

Did she have to use the word 'taken' as if I were an invader who'd come and dispossessed some starving serf?

'I've only got half a house.'

'The Durocs' house?'

'That's right, you know it!'

'Of course I do!'

Then we talked about the local footpaths, the neighbours (she knew the Malebranches), the *mairie*, the school and the church. We went all the way round the village, in fact. I had to find something else to say.

'Are you staying for the party this evening?'

'Which party?'

I turned to Sue, with pleading eyes like an English gun dog, and, given that she was sweetness itself in everything connected with parties, drinking sessions, Irish groups from Bobigny and the like, she replied 'Yes, I was going to invite you, but he didn't give me a chance.'

'Well, yes, then.'

And I nodded my head from Martine to Sue with all the gratitude of an English gun dog for his master.

I took a swig of whisky and the image of the dead man loomed again.

'So do you know the Caminades, then?'

Her expression changed as if we'd suddenly started talking shop.

'Yes. I know them only too well.'

I then understood that, once again, I'd do better to change the subject. And now Sue took control of the situation. My face must have darkened, all the same, as I accumulated all these questions I wanted to ask her sooner or later about this place that she knew so well and in which I lived. Why did I have to keep thinking about bodies when I was looking at a perfectly attractive young woman who'd given me a very provocative smile at the outset?

'Sue,' I said, interrupting her, 'could I have another whisky?'

She replied with a 'hmm, hmm' and a raised eyebrow, although she addressed them more to Martine than to me.

Then she told me that Martine's great-uncle, who'd died some years earlier, had been a curate with a passion for local history, a local publishing company had even published a book of his that was still read to this day in which he chronicled all the tittle-tattle of an ecclesiastical or more general nature in the region.

'My great-uncle was a mine of information,' explained Martine, adjusting her black hair-band. 'Every Sunday after Mass, my parents and I would have lunch with him and he would tell us all about the various villages, the châteaux and the people. Amazing stories, he could even tell us about the Hundred Years War,' she said. (Then she paused as if, remembering that we were English, she thought she'd made a gaffe.) 'Well, all sorts of stories, anyway, even without the war.'

'Which war?'

'The last war.'

I exchanged glances with Sue. The war. The subject and the source of every problem in the French countryside. Every year at Christmas, all through my childhood, I would watch *The Battle of Britain*, for instance, over and over again, or a film about the Royal Navy or the Desert Rats. By living in France, I'd discovered that the last war had been something quite different and had left scars on the ground that could no longer be seen in the skies over the English Channel where the Spitfires had come spiralling down in flames. Even the plaque on the rival café to Sue's, which recalled Buckmaster's presence here, spoke about the torture, the betrayal and the struggle of the *Maquis*. And the English of the Dordogne had got into the habit of listening without interrupting whenever the locals spoke about the war in front of them. They didn't talk about Churchill, Montgomery or the RAF, they talked about quite different things, darker things, more shameful perhaps, and heroic too, but things that had happened clandestinely rather than out in the open in the sky or the desert. As if to confirm this, Martine then added 'Plenty of things went on in La Berthonie during the war.'

The image of that young peasant's body all in his Sunday best came back to me as did the pictures conjured up by the numerous accounts I'd heard of his brother's death in the lake near Nontron. Could it be that these deaths were actually caused by something that went all that far back? It was absurd. The region had had its fill of account-settling and I preferred not to know about it all.

The model was getting dressed again and the artists had

come out of their little room to have a drink. Thompson, redder than ever, led the way. He came into the bar regaling us with a dirty joke, which wasn't like him at all but — having taken into account the combined effect of his solitude and the fact that he'd just spent the afternoon in front of a naked woman with an enormous bosom — he was forgiven. She herself was following closely behind him, calling out to Sue 'A white wine please, love, I think I've earned it!'

Johnny made his appearance next, along with Marianne, he came over to Martine and set about chatting her up quite shamelessly. She obviously thought he was very common (him — the genuine aristocrat!) and turned back to me, an authentic *petit bourgeois*, because she obviously found me more acceptable. Questions of class are, after all, a major preoccupation for the English.

Other guests who had not taken part in the art class started to arrive, like that caricature of a Scotsman who went by the name of Gordon, at least six foot four with curly red hair, a great throaty laugh and a habit of drinking half-litres of beer as if it were lemonade. He spoke very loudly, rolling his r's, as he talked about the Scottish rugby team and their exploits in the Five Nations Cup. Like all French people, Martine hadn't grasped the fact that there was a relatively important difference between Scotland and England and she asked him a host of questions about 'the English' as if he were one of their number. And Gordon, who was trying to keep his calm, went redder in the face with each of Martine's interventions. Realising that he was about to snap, he turned away to talk to the Irish fiddler from the outskirts of Paris, fully believing that he was dealing with a fellow Celt.

'These Scots!' I said with an amused and condescending smile and then added 'Is your great-uncle still alive? The one who wrote this book.'

'Oh, no, he died several years ago now, but I remember him

really clearly.' (Sue had already told me this, but I'd forgotten.) 'I'll give you a copy of his book if you like . . . if you'd be interested.'

'Absolutely completely,' I replied, still playing the card of the gentleman abroad who, being exquisitely elegant, wouldn't know how to speak any language correctly other than his own. 'Would you bring it over for me?'

She looked up with a slight smile.

'Why not?'

'Do you have a car?'

'I borrow my father's when I'm here. I live in Bordeaux most of the time, I'm studying law and I don't really need one there.'

'I haven't got a car. Once I'd bought my house, there wasn't any money left for one, so I get about on a *mobylette*.'

She started literally howling with laughter, and this detail about my mode of transport meant that she could pigeon-hole me into another category, one that was highly prized at the faculty of law in Bordeaux, that of the 'eccentric Englishman'. I'd won the hand, so to speak, but I had to be careful not to go over the top.

The evening went off as planned, by eleven o'clock everyone was blind drunk, dancing through a fug of cigarette smoke which stood in for the Irish mist, people were shouting and laughing, Johnny was dancing with Sue, Thompson kept shaking his head despairingly while still managing to enjoy himself. Marianne was screeching anecdotes about her nanny and then she started to cry while she told the Scotsman that her dog, a hideous and aggressive mongrel, had died the previous summer in circumstances too appalling for her to describe.

Martine had left earlier and in a more sober state, taking with her my telephone number and I sat smiling at the beams across the ceiling.

Louis Sanders

When they started spinning, at about two or three in the morning, I decided the time had come to get onto my *mobylette* and to head back to La Berthonie.

4

I don't really remember which side of the road I was on, but the roads in the Dordogne are hardly busy at that time of night. They're completely dark. And sometimes, without really seeing it, I could sense the white wings of a barn owl flying overhead. It was appallingly cold and I thought that my hands would stick to the handlebars because of the ice. The engine made a deafening noise, like a chain-saw, and with my senses atrophied by the alcohol, I felt as if the trees along the side of the road were going to fall in and crush me. And I would lie there screaming like a madman with no one to hear me except for a few animals startled from their sleep, who would scamper away with a rustling of leaves. When I reached a large lake in front of a château on the road to La Berthonie, I stopped to look at the dark motionless water which dictated its imposing silence on the surrounding countryside. I sat there on the seat of my *mobylette*, as if to catch my breath, as if — rather than being carried — I'd run all the way there. In the distance, on the other side of the lake, I could make out the perfectly black silhouette of the château against the dark blue sky that was strewn with countless stars. I'd never seen so many stars as on those Dordogne nights. The château belonged to some Dutch people, a very rich old lady and her son who lived with her. People said they no longer talked to each other, that they hated each other but had nowhere else to go. They also said that the son was useless and stayed there so that he could sponge off his mother, and

that she never stopped reminding him he was a failure, condemned to depending on the one person he cared for and who
felt for him a withering contempt tempered by a thoroughly
compromised sort of affection. It was Sue who had told me
about them, because she used to go and see them, separately of
course, but quite often. She'd also told me that the château, a
place with no real character, was built in the nineteenth century
and had been used as a prison during the war. The Germans had
locked up members of the Resistance there and, to escape torture, the prisoners had thrown themselves out of the upper windows. Sue insisted that the old Dutchwoman hadn't even taken
the trouble to remove the copper numbers that were nailed to
the bedroom doors when they had been cells. How many bodies lay at the bottom of the lake? I imagined the body of the
dead man's brother, floating like a log on a surface as calm and
dark as this, coming back from a trip round all the seediest cafés
in Angoulême, a body swollen with water and alcohol, quite
unrecognisable.

Alcohol, the dreaded alcohol, I'd drunk enough of it for
there to be absolutely no relationship between time, action and
distance; each existed independently of the others and it was
this independence which meant that suddenly, just like that,
at the end of a road which I knew like the back of my hand I
saw my own house, as if in a dream. I must have left the *mobylette*
on its side, because that was how I found it the following morning or, to be more precise, early the following afternoon when
I woke up. I went into my house, not, it has to be said, with any
reassuring feeling of being somewhere that belonged to me.
Especially because by then I'd quite convinced myself, as if the
slumbering countryside had been whispering it in my ear, that
the two brothers — the one who'd drowned and the one who'd
been crushed to death — had not died accidental deaths: they
had been killed. And in the state that I was in there was no
shortage of ghosts either in what I called the sitting room or

on the staircase or, when I got there, in my bedroom or even next to my bed. I knocked into so many things as I staggered about that I thought the room must have at least six walls.

By some extraordinary miracle, I didn't have any dreams. The first thing I thought about when I woke up was my headache, the second was Martine and the third was the Dordogne. As I made my way over to the window to look out once again onto the same leafless tree, I asked myself what I was doing there. And it was then that I saw the old Dutchwoman walking in her slow, steady way towards the track that led down into the dell to Pisse-Chèvre. She came right past the house and she looked up, saw my shadow through the window and looked away quickly as if I'd caught her red-handed doing something wrong, then she continued on her way, a little faster than before. But why was she going to Pisse-Chèvre? And was she really going there? I'd forgotten to ask the Malebranches about her. And why should I have done? As a widow, didn't she have a right to live on her own if that was what she wanted? As I did myself, when it came down to it. The fact was, I probably wanted to get to know these people to break the monotony: her and the Englishman from Pisse-Chèvre who didn't even say hello to anyone but who, despite everything that was said about him, had won the approval of the Malebranches.

*

'Poor thing, tch,' said Madame Malebranche, 'that's no life, living all alone looking after your son.'

'Looking after?'

'Yes, he never goes out, he stays in his room with his shutters closed all day, but when he does get out . . . Oh, my goodness! He's the very devil.'

'She should put him in an institution, I dunno,' added old

man Malebranche. 'Like the Caminades did with their daughter, come to think of it.'

'Why, what's wrong with him?'

'Well, he's mad isn't he? Traumatised, that's what the doctor said. There's a doctor who comes sometimes. It's not that he'd do anyone much harm, poor thing. But tch! Can't do anything about it.'

'Traumatised,' old man Malebranche reiterated doubtfully. 'He wasn't ever really normal, anyway. Sometimes he gets out from the château there and she has to run all over the place trying to catch him again.'

'But you can't do anything about it.'

'How old is he?'

'Oh, he must be about thirty.'

'About that. But he's built like an ox. Haven't you ever seen him?'

'No.'

'Well, there you are, you're better off not.'

François came into the kitchen then, having finished some exhausting task. He was smiling and nodding his head towards me . . .

'We were telling Mr . . . Mr . . . about the old Dutchwoman.'

'Oh, yes . . . yes . . . what sort of life is that!'

'Yup.'

'And what was it that traumatised him?'

'No one really knows.'

'I think they say he saw an accident once and that someone died in the accident and that he's never been the same since.'

'And who died?'

'Hmm, well . . .'

'Can't be sure. That's what they say.'

'Who says?'

'Hmm, well . . .'

'Doesn't she talk to anyone about it?'

'Just to the doctor and he, well, he doesn't talk about it.'

'Well, course not, it's a professional secret. Will you have something to drink, Mr . . .'

'Just a little one, then,' I replied while my heart sank at the thought of ingesting their alcoholised sugar, and to think that just a few hours earlier I'd promised myself that I would no longer drink anything other than carrot juice.

In the end, the undrinkable *pineau* actually did me some good.

'Doesn't she come to see you?'

'Never.'

Someone knocked at the door.

'Come in!' cried Madame Malebranche.

A stocky character in blue overalls appeared in the doorway of the room and took off his beret before greeting us all in patois. Old man Malebranche threw him a 'Ko vaï?' which means 'How are you?', then they exchanged a few words, still in patois which I obviously didn't understand. After a few nods of the head all round, he sat down on the seat opposite me. He must have been about seventy-five, but it was hard to tell because he seemed ageless, like all the local peasants.

I grasped what must have been explained to him in patois, because he turned to me and said 'So you're the Englishman from La Berthonie, you live next door to Duroc.'

This sentence hit me like a slap in the face. The Englishman from La Berthonie. There was the Englishman from Pisse-Chèvre, the madman. There was the old Dutchwoman, the widow, and now I was the Englishman from La Berthonie. God alone knew what other qualifying phrase or peculiarity this definition might be embellished with. The idiot? the confirmed bachelor? the slacker?

'So you like it in our country, then?' he asked.

'Very much.'

Did he really have to say in 'our' country? As if to remind

me that I was not in my own country? But he didn't lose any time reassuring me that there was nothing xenophobic about him.

'I remember we had an English officer with us when I was in the *Maquis*.'

The locals don't talk about the Resistance, they always call it the *Maquis* which actually means scrubland, even if there wasn't any scrub in the area, only woodland.

'Were you in the *Maquis*?'

'Hey?'

'Were you in the *Maquis*?'

'Yes. I went in at fourteen. To follow my brother who didn't want to do forced labour. So I joined him.'

I'd often wondered how many people would have joined the Resistance if the Nazis hadn't introduced forced labour in France.

'You got all sorts in the *Maquis*,' he went on. 'I was a machine-gun server. The man as was firing it was Spanish. International brigades, you see. He'd come back through this bit of country and he'd already been fighting for four years, that one. He used to say "If you is hurt, me killing you. No talking."'

Then he burst out laughing, turning towards old man Malebranche as if no one had ever told him anything so funny. Old man Malebranche, who must have heard this story a hundred times and who would have preferred to talk about the milk yield or the cold weather for the time of year, just shrugged his shoulders. But it was too late, the visitor had embarked on his reminiscences.

'He was always the one who did the killing, the Spaniard. One day we went to blow up the locomotives at the depot in Périgueux. There was someone on sentry duty. It was the Spaniard who slipped over the wall. He was very agile. One cut of the knife, not a sound, we didn't hear another thing. But the officer, the one who'd taught us how to use our weapons and who was in charge of all the operations, he was an Englishman . . . like you, you see.'

'Wouldn't want to go through times like that again. When everyone's killing everyone,' commented old man Malebranche.

He felt a vague resentment listening to these accounts of heroic acts, because he himself had not participated in any way. Or barely. In 1945 someone had come to find him on his farm and had put a gun in his hand. He was put on guard and ordered to shoot anyone either wearing a German uniform or from the *Milice*. No such person had made an appearance and, for him, the war had begun and ended like that. Even old mother Malebranche felt mildly irritated seeing her guest trotting out his 'old stories'.

'The members of the *Milice* were even worse than the Germans, you see. We were even more frightened of them. But the English had given us bombs. No bigger than a pin. You detonated the thing, slipped it into a collaborator's pocket, when you were talking to him in the café, for example, and bang! it exploded a quarter of an hour later. It was the English who gave us those, you see . . .'

And he burst out laughing again as if these delayed bombs struck him as a good example of what people call the English sense of humour. Actually, I was quite grateful to him for thinking that there was any connection between myself and these heroic predecessors who'd risked their lives to help the Resistance.

'Wouldn't want to go through times like that again,' repeated old man Malebranche, shrugging his shoulders.

Realising that it was now time to stop, the other man agreed with a succinct 'Ohhh, no,' leaving me hungry for more, to use a woefully inadequate expression.

The conversation about the cows and the weather for the time of year could at last go ahead. I listened politely as I mentally replayed the images that the tales of murderous Spaniards and SAS men on operations had conjured up in my mind.

I discovered almost by chance that this man was called Marcel. He drained his glass in one go, having not touched it all the time he'd been there.

'Right, I must get back to it,' he said and he got up.

I made the most of the opportunity by doing the same and adding 'I'll go with you.'

'Well, then, till next time,' Madame Malebranche said to me.

'Why don't you come over and see me some time for a quick one?'

'Oh, it's just, when you're busy . . .'

She didn't finish her sentence.

Marcel and I then both saw the silhouette of the old Dutchwoman passing the gate at the end of the Malebranches' rutted and bumpy yard, we saw her from behind as she cut across the field and headed back up the hill towards the château on the other side.

Marcel stared at this tiny distant figure with her little hat and he shook his head compassionately.

'Do you know her? The Dutchwoman?'

He turned round sharply as if he'd forgotten I was there, as if my voice had suddenly brought him back down to earth.

'Who?'

'The Dutchwoman?'

'You mean Rachel? Over there? She's not Dutch. I know that's what they call her, but she's not Dutch.'

5

'You see there are things that people round here don't like to remember. Always to do with the war. And there are some that made money out of it.'

'You mean the Malebranches?'

'No, no, not them. They didn't have anything to do with it, poor things. I don't even know if you could hold it against them. That's just the way they are. No, there were some people who informed on others, you see. They'd go to the *Milice* office in Périgueux and they'd be given money. Rachel isn't Dutch, she's a Jew.'

I thought I could see the obscure link between the two parts of this explanation; I also thought of telling him that being Dutch and being Jewish were not mutually exclusive, but I thought it better to let him go on.

'D'you know, I still know some people in the area who've got savings from that particular line of business.'

'Who?'

'Oh, come on, I couldn't really tell you that, could I! But it's not far from here. And they should have been made to pay. There are some that paid dearly for it, mark my words. Not dearly enough, mind you,' he added with a new edge of vehemence in his voice. 'I lost friends too, you know. And poor Rachel, in her case . . .'

'What happened to her?'

'Do you want me to tell you?'

'Yes. Of course. Would you like to come over to my house?'

And, perhaps because I was English, he trusted me. The memories of an officer who was an expert with a Bren gun . . .

★

'You see, Rachel was Mr Weil's daughter. There were four sisters. Mr Weil was a Jew from Alsace who fled here with his whole family because this was still in the unoccupied zone at the time.'

He was sitting at my table, turning his glass between his fingers and looking round the room to gauge my character from my belongings.

'Before the war we didn't know who was a Jew, who was Protestant and who was Catholic. We didn't give a fig. We were all socialists in my family, we didn't go to church. Then, when they came over from Alsace, they started saying "So and so's Protestant, such and such is Jewish, etc." Then, as you know, the Germans came into the unoccupied zone. And things became difficult. Some went to join the *Maquis*, others the *Milice*, and I — well, like I told you, I followed my brother. We lived in hiding and the Weils lived in hiding too. Then Weil joined our network and his wife and daughters lived in a hay barn. You had to make sure you never showed your face and you had to change your hiding place pretty regularly. Because of the informers. Then someone informed on our whole network. Mind you, she didn't live long enough to enjoy the money. But she told the *Milice* everything, the bitch, including where the Weil girls were hiding. And the worst of it is that the woman who did this was the mother of one of the boys in our network and she didn't even know it. I was with Weil when the *Milice* came to nab us, we were running for the woods, we'd almost made it, the Spaniard was ahead of us, we knew that once we were in the woods we'd be safe, but Weil suddenly stopped and I thought I heard him say "my wife . . ." as he stopped. And I've often thought about that. I just turned to look at him, standing there with his hands hanging by his sides and the *Milice* closing in on him. Then he slumped to the ground, he'd been shot in the back. I've often wondered why he stopped like that. He must have been worrying about his wife, I don't know. In a situation like that you don't always react the way you'd expect. All he said was "my wife . . ." but, while all this was going on, his wife had been warned that they were coming to get them. That the soldiers were on their way, Germans this time. She was clever, that woman, you know. Do you know what she did? She told her daughters to take all their clothes off, there they were, all four of them with nothing on, Rachel and her sisters. And Mrs Weil took great handfuls of stinging nettles and beat the girls' bodies with them. Soon they were red all over, covered in little spots. They were just children at the time, except for the eldest who must have been about eighteen. When the Germans arrived, she showed them her daughters and said "Yes, you can take us, but look, we're contagious!" They looked at the girls with their red arms and legs and faces covered in spots. They were frightened. The officer even told his soldiers not to go into the room. And so they left.'

He lifted up his fist which had been resting on the table and brought it back down again. Then he raised his eyebrows and nodded several times.

'You see, eh?'

'And then?'

'Then?'

'Yes, what happened then?'

'Oh, well, they carried on hiding till the end of the war which wasn't that far off. In the end it was the collaborators' turn to be frightened. But Mrs Weil never really got over her husband's death. She had a nervous breakdown, if that's what they call it. And, anyway, bringing up four girls all alone . . . In the end she died. Died of grief, you might say. Not all of the girls left. The eldest got married quite quickly to a man from Nontron. She still lives in Périgueux. The other two went to Paris, I think, or perhaps even to America, I don't know. And then there's Rachel who lives here.'

'Does the one who lives in Périgueux come and see her sister?'

'I wouldn't know.'

'Do you ever go and see her?'

He hesitated for a moment.

'No. Rachel and I are about the same age, you know, and I saw her growing up and I liked what I saw,' he explained with a half smile and a shrug of his shoulders. 'You know what it's like. Then she got married too, to the Dutchman, a very rich man who came to live in the area and bought the château. He was much older than her and he'd apparently been in a concentration camp. In Germany. It left him terribly weak. But they still managed to live together for a while, they must have been happy.'

'From what I've been told, they had a son.'

'Poor Rachel, yes, they had a son. A good, sturdy boy. But it's up here that he's not so strong,' he said, pointing to his temple. 'Too highly strung apparently. Yes, poor Rachel.'

Like the last time, he downed his drink in one, clapped the glass down noisily, wiped his mouth on the back of his hand and — after a variety of comments along the lines of 'Well, that's life' and 'Not much you can do about it' — he made his way to the door. He walked with a hunch and with his beret planted over his perfectly square neck and I was absolutely incapable of imagining him as a young man running for cover in the woods, carrying a machine gun or a simple shotgun and taking orders from an Englishman from Sandhurst dressed up as a peasant. He turned round, held out his hand and asked whether I'd like to drop in for a drink sometime if I just happened to be in his village. I watched him all the way to the bend in the track as he headed back to his car. I heard the sound of an old engine, then I saw the Renault 4 appearing from behind the ruined manor house known as 'The Pavilion' in the middle of the village. But then all the peasants have Renault 4s.

*

I poured myself some more of the Bergerac after he'd left and went over to the armchair next to the cold fireplace. The locals never sit in my armchairs, as if they were afraid it was somehow obscene to sink into the cushions. They always preferred hard, wooden chairs or, even better, a bench, but I haven't got one.

The silence had changed and the frequent noises that punctuated it made me think some intense human activity was going on in secret somewhere and that it was this activity rather than the wind which was causing the leaves to rustle, the branches to sway and the odd bird to fly off in fright. As if I were waiting to hear a gunshot, a cry, an order called out in the middle of a field or across a hillside. Then cries of pain, injured men or naked girls whipped by stinging nettles, covering their faces and crying. I kept hoping, in vain, that I would hear the sound of another car, one of those impromptu visits that are so common in the country, someone who just happened to be passing, one of my English friends, for example, hoping to be offered a drink, even if they — unlike the locals — are more likely to give some advance warning. And failing that, a telephone call inviting me to another party, but we'd just had one the day before. Martine perhaps? It was too soon, she couldn't in all decency ring the very day after meeting me, I might have drawn a few conclusions . . . She'd wait at least a week, she'd find an excuse, even if, at the end of the day, she was drawing the same conclusions. Better to respect the various conventions, however much they contradicted each other.

I took the sketches I'd made the day before out of my folder and had a look at them, wondering if I could make anything of them. In the end, no, nothing to be had from them. Polish off the Bergerac. Maybe. It was at times like this that I came back to the same question, one which raised its head far too frequently in winter: 'What on earth am I doing here?' The old boy's tales of the Resistance were still ringing in my head, conjuring up pictures; for once, I was seeing an episode of the war in colour and not in black and white as it appeared in the archive film that you see on television in England. There was the dark blue of his beret, so dark it was almost black, the *feldgrau* of the German uniforms, the red of a beaten body, of the blood trickling from Weil's wounds. These images mingled with scenes from the funeral vigil, as if it were the old Dutchwoman's father, killed by the *Milice*, whom I'd seen lying dead on his bed. And the Malebranches standing there shrugging, saying 'Wouldn't want to go through that again'. But I was going through it all again, all jumbled up. Another glass of Bergerac and the list of what I could be doing spooled through my mind, but each different activity, each distraction, seemed like some onerous chore, starting with lighting the fire so that I could sit in the chair in comfort and read some English story which would help me forget all my suspicions. I'd so convinced myself that the young peasant had been killed that I almost felt frightened, as if the murderer were crouching in the vegetation outside, as if I were his next victim, as if — in fact — this prospect might save me from the boredom which was making me ill. It was all the more maddening because, for the first time in my life, I was doing what I'd always wanted to do, which was, in a word: nothing.

I'd sold my house in Hackney two years earlier, after splitting up with my then partner whom I'd met at university and who, I'm told, has since married an obscenely rich lawyer, a Trinity man like myself, whom I vaguely knew and never liked that much. My instincts were obviously not far wrong.

The difference in property prices between East London and

the French countryside meant that I could afford this house — or half house — and still have enough cash to live meagrely for two or three years and dedicate myself to my real passion, painting. After that . . .

But for now, I'd have liked to press a button on a remote control and rewind my life like a video, to have gone back to Hackney and to have explained to my then partner that etc., etc.

I started shivering with cold. I got up, fully intending to get some logs from the barn. The barn seemed too far and the wood too heavy. The gas bottle for the heater was empty, it was too early to go to bed and the prospect of ending up between the sheets in the middle of the afternoon was extremely depressing.

By five o'clock, night had fallen and everything outside was in darkness. The Bergerac was finished, but the fact that it was dark meant that I could have a glass of whisky without feeling too guilty. I vaguely thought that my voice shouldn't be too slurred when Martine rang. But that particular danger struck me as being very remote.

It was after the second glass that I thought I heard noises in the other half of the house, which — given the state that I was in — was not at all surprising. I went out into the freezing air to have a quick look round the outside walls, which was obviously pointless. The sound, somewhere between a scratching noise, a footstep and a breath, can only really have happened inside my head, one of those noises that doesn't exist and which you think you hear after funeral vigils, after stories of betrayal and loneliness and of widows with mad sons.

And yet . . . I thought I detected a movement through the window. It was only the Virginia creeper over the window moving in the wind like an arm. Then suddenly, someone shouted. A woman's voice, someone I didn't know, but there was something distinguished about the voice, despite the fact that it teetered between fear and hysteria. A voice that managed to keep its note of authority as it called out 'Come back! Come back now!' Then the sound of footsteps, a frantic chase, feet scattering the pebbles on the path.

I got up and stood absolutely motionless in the middle of the room with my glass in my hand, like a guest at a cocktail party who suddenly finds they've got no one to talk to. I didn't dare go over to the door to see what was going on. At the time I was quite sure that I would witness another murder. Then, the next minute, the engine sound that I'd been waiting for all day finally arrived, followed by a screech of tyres, a door being slammed, then more footsteps — more sprightly this time, more energetic. A man running. Dogs had started barking all over the village.

I was ashamed of my cowardice and, like an English officer who'd parachuted in to lead a group of Resistance fighters, I strode out into the night, putting on the outside light. Just over to my left I saw a little black Fiat, empty. The shouting and the noise had moved away, it now only came in snatches. A man's voice, firm but reassuring, mingled with the pleading from an elderly woman who — I had deduced, although I couldn't be absolutely sure — was the old Dutchwoman. (I did now know that she wasn't born in the Netherlands, but I could no longer think of her in any other terms.) A few minutes later I heard the man's voice saying 'Come on, come on, that's enough now', with a slight local accent that was immediately apparent on a few telltale syllables. They were coming closer, but I still couldn't see them. I noticed that François Malebranche was at the far end of the track, beyond the Fiat, and was standing with his hands on his hips, nodding his head, implying both helplessness and compassion. The only sound now was the dogs barking and even they eventually fell silent. I was somehow reassured by the fact that the Malebranches' son was there. He gave such an impression of strength and steadiness that I regained my confidence and managed to convince myself that the situation was well in hand and that nothing supernatural or bloodthirsty was going to happen. A light went out at one of the windows of a house that belonged to another widow, a little way up the hill. François Malebranche trudged off and the village settled back into silence, as if he'd come out of his house to put an end to the commotion and the whole night had obeyed him.

About half an hour later, I heard footsteps again, the regular, steady paces of a man who knew where he was going and was probably heading for home at the end of the day.

It was in fact a dark-haired, athletic, young-looking man of about forty; from his suede jacket, his jeans and his loafers, it was clear that he wasn't a farmworker. He was heading for the black Fiat and talking to himself, saying 'Well, well, well, what a day!'

He was the one I'd heard talking and calling earlier with the old Dutchwoman.

'Good evening,' I said before he'd actually seen me.

He almost gave a start and, when he turned round, I realised that he couldn't make out my face.

He stopped and returned the greeting, imitating my calm, measured tone which was completely incongruous given the circumstances. Then he came over, looking slightly amused.

'Are you the Englishman?'

'Yes, I am. The Englishman from La Berthonie. The one from Pisse-Chèvre is further on down.'

'Yes, I know, I know,' he replied laughing and then added, 'well, I never, things certainly happen in this little spot. Round Pisse-Chèvre.'

I hadn't been of that opinion during the course of the day, but now I had to concede that he was right.

He was obviously from the area, but went on laughing about the name 'Pisse-Chèvre' to which I'd become immune, no longer finding it especially funny.

'I'm the doctor,' he explained, before I'd had time to ask him anything.

'Would you like a drink?'

He hesitated for a moment, then smiled again.

'Why not, if you're offering.'

He noticed the bottle of whisky inside on the table and, making a sweeping movement in its general direction, he announced 'Now, that would fit the bill.'

Then he sat down in one of the armchairs, even though I hadn't really invited him to, and he waited to be given his drink.

'It's not very warm in your house. Don't you have central heating?'

'No.'

'You don't get ill much, do you? You've never come to my surgery.'

'No.'

'The English are never ill. Of the ones that live here, the few who've ever been to see me had really serious problems. They tend to tell themselves that, if it's not serious, it'll sort itself out on its own and, if it's serious, there's nothing you can do about it. Am I right?'

'Maybe.'

I was rather embarrassed with myself for appearing so untalkative when I was the one who'd asked him in for a drink, but I didn't feel like making small talk with him. I had just one burning question and it eventually came out.

'What happened this evening? I heard all sorts of things going on.'

'That doesn't surprise me. It's always the same, old Mrs Krug's son, he's mad. He stays shut up in his room all day for weeks on end. Someone must have told you all this.'

'Yes, some of it. Did he escape?'

'Sometimes, when she's not there, he gets out through the window. It's a drop of more than two metres. He's never sprained his ankle. He's never hurt himself. That's because he's mad. He always manages to get away without a scratch on him. Then he runs about all over the place, not knowing whether he's coming or going. Then his mother sets off after him, it can go on for hours and, in the end, one of the neighbours rings me, even in the middle of the night.

'The son usually listens to me and, given that his condition makes him ten times as strong as a normal man, it's just as well. I had a really hard time getting him back once, he was fighting like a . . .'

He was going to say a madman, but he seemed to prefer stopping at that.

'And what exactly is wrong with him?'

'Oh, all sorts of things. He's obsessed by morbid thoughts. Thoughts of murder. This whisky of yours is very good, by the way. Is it single malt?'

'Help yourself to some more.'

'Thank you. They say he witnessed a murder when he was in his teens. But obviously, if you listen to all the stories people tell . . .'

'Even the story about his mother? The nettles, the Germans, all that?'

'Oh, you know about that? You've certainly integrated your-self here,' he said with a laugh. 'No, that's actually true. Mind you, even this story about a murder is perfectly possible.'

'That he witnessed it?'

'Yes.'

'But wasn't there an inquiry?'

'Based on the testimony of a madman?'

'But they must have found a body?'

'Yes, but they couldn't prove that he was there, the madman, I mean. Perhaps he heard people talking about it. And it's not far from here, so he knows the places concerned and he has a fertile imagination, you know. It looked more like a suicide. It wasn't me who dealt with it.'

He didn't say any more about it, even though he obviously wanted to talk. He swirled the whisky in the bottom of his glass, pursing his lips and raising his eyebrows. It was clear from the way he sighed that he was exhausted. Then he suddenly muttered: 'And what if he'd seen the other one . . .'

'Which other one?'

'Sorry?'

He looked up and bit his lip, as if suddenly realising that he'd let something slip out.

'Oh, nothing, just more stories. There's no shortage of them round you here, at Pisse-Chèvre,' he said, hoping that these two words would, yet again, serve as a joke and that we would start talking about something else, laughing together about the improbable names you come across in the French countryside.

'Did you do these?' he asked, pointing at my sketches which were still on the table.

'Yes.'

'Are you a painter?'

'Oh, when it suits me.'

'I collect drawings. Particularly seventeenth- and eighteenth-century, but you have to go to Bordeaux to find anything. I've also got a few by contemporary artists, mind you. Old Mrs Krug has the most amazing collection at the château. Have you ever been there?'

'No, never.'

'Her husband built up the collection and brought it over from Holland. They've got some Dutch old masters. In the hall, for example, there are some magnificent sixteenth-century *danses macabres.*'

Of course. At least the theme of this painting in the hall meant that I could return to the subject that the doctor had deliberately dropped a little earlier.

'You mentioned another. Another what? Another murder?'

He shrugged his shoulders. Then, in the end, as if he'd come to a decision, he looked me squarely in the eye, drank a mouthful of whisky and announced 'Yes, another murder.'

'When?'

'Recently.'

'Where?'

'Near here, everything happens round La Berthonie and Pisse-Chèvre, you know that perfectly well,' he said with a smile that was slightly less amused than before.

'Do you mean the Caminades' son who was found under a tree?'

I was almost excited at the thought of seeing my suspicions confirmed by a man of science like the local doctor.

'Yes, that's who I mean.'

'But, they're saying it was an accident.'

'I know, it was even I who said it.'

'So?'

'So . . . I don't know why I'm telling you all this. I shouldn't.'

'I'm not from the area.'

'That's not enough of a reason. Anyway, I've already said too much, it's because I'm so tired. I can't go on. And then your whisky. Mind you, I've pretty much had enough of the whole business.'

'What business?'

'There were signs that the man had been struck on the head and body.'

'You couldn't see them.'

'How do you know?'

'I went to the vigil.'

'Oh yes. That's the work of the undertakers. They do a good job. Either way, what I saw couldn't have been done by a falling tree.'

'And what could have done it?'

'He'd been struck, as I say. With a club, even a branch that happened to be to hand. Anything. A tool, not a very sharp one, mind you.'

'The family saw the body. Didn't they ask any questions?'

'Not out loud, at least.'

'But how come?'

'It goes back a long way, I tell you.'

'What does it go back to?'

'Even I don't know all of it and, anyway, there's more than enough with what we've got. Come on, I'm not going to tell you everything. I can't believe I've been so stupid. I'm beginning to wonder who really is the madman. But please don't talk to anyone about this. Especially not the Malebranches, for example. You'll have to keep it quiet. Okay?'

'Yes, of course.'

Then he got up slowly as if his limbs were cripplingly stiff.

'Thank you for the whisky, anyway. It was very good . . . single malt . . . Come and see me when you're ill. It would be a pleasure, if I can say that, and then I could show you my collection of drawings. You know, there are some really beautiful collections from the Italian Renaissance in England, all the best work is over there, did you know that?'

'So it seems.'

I didn't particularly feel like falling ill or admiring any *danses macabres*, I'd got one of my own devising rattling around in my head, making the most infernal racket.

It was four o'clock in the morning the last time I looked at the alarm clock on my bedside table before falling asleep.

6

I was woken by the February sun. When it shines, it's always warm and even in the depths of winter you can sit out in the sunshine in the middle of the day and have a drink. It's at times like that that you don't regret being here. Winter becomes confused with the illusion of spring for a few hours, before night falls.

I thought back over the previous evening's improbable scene as I made myself a cup of instant coffee and lit my first cigarette of the day, then I thought of the doctor's confessions to me, a complete stranger, but what did he have to lose? How could I, a stranger, a vague English painter who lived on his own in the middle of nowhere, go and tell the police that the Caminades' son wasn't actually crushed by a tree and the doctor hadn't said anything because this or that and that the old Dutchwoman and that the Weil father's death and that . . . and that . . . They would have looked at me with the same amused consternation as if I tried to tell them that Lady Diana had been killed by the secret service. I could have told the Malebranches, obviously, but their attitude would have been that it was none of my business anyway. I could have told the whole story to the English who lived here. But what for? The consequences of the whole affair had as much bearing on them as they would if I'd conducted a conference on the subject in the library of a private club in Soho. I poured a lot of milk into my all but transparent coffee and went and sat on the squarely-fashioned teak bench that had been donated to a public park in Sheffield by a certain Winterbottom and which had ended up in a second-hand furniture dealers' in Camden Lock. A little copper plaque in the middle of the back-rest still bore testimony to Mr Winterbottom's generosity towards the parks and gardens of Sheffield. Amidst this general calm, I could hear one of the Malebranches' agricultural machines being started up somewhere just behind the house. It was the one they used to clear out the muck from the cow stalls and to build an impressive pile of the stuff in front of the absolutely hideous breeze-block building which they'd erected to shelter their cows and which I could unfortunately see when I went to sit under the enormous walnut tree in the middle of the lawn.

It was to some extent thanks to this disagreeable din, accompanied by the rather more agreeable smell of fresh cow dung, that I decided to go back into the kitchen, which meant that I didn't miss the lovely Martine's telephone call.

I didn't recognise her voice straight away because I wasn't expecting to hear it so soon, but I managed to keep my composure, which struck me as essential in the circumstances because, when we'd first met she'd talked enthusiastically about a few English writers and two or three perfectly ridiculous American films about the English, Cambridge and the big country houses where people play croquet, all of which added up to a sort of Ralph Lauren catalogue about as close to the reality of my dear country as Maurice Chevalier was to the Malebranches. This composure had to win over my quite natural nervousness, but still had to stay within the limits of courtesy and of the pleasure I felt to be speaking to her.

'Did you get home late the other night?'

'Not very, just after you,' I lied, to suggest that in her absence the evening had lost all its charm.

Then, after a rather weighty silence, I added 'Are you still in the area?'

She'd said she was staying for a month.

'Yes.'

'Are you very busy?'

'No, not particularly.'

'Oh, really? What would you say to coming and having a cup of tea with me at five o'clock?'

I wondered then whether I was overdoing it a bit with the folklore, but it didn't seem to have bothered her. I even thought I could hear her smiling in amusement on the other end of the line.

'You did say you have the use of a car, didn't you?'

'Yes.'

'And you know the way, don't you?'

'Of course, I told you that I spent my whole childhood near where you are.'

'Yes, yes, of course, I remember.'

I hesitated before throwing, for example, the odd charming syntactical error into the conversation and then decided that it would be pointless.

She'd hardly hung up before I started hurtling about, picking up stray socks, emptying ashtrays, clearing away the sketches of the cut-and-blow-dryer who was still lying naked on my table, changing my shirt, having a shave, etc. Should I change the sheets? No, too presumptuous, on the other hand it would certainly not go amiss to run the Hoover over the place, something that hadn't been done for a good month. Reinstate the picture of the Trinity Rugby Fifteen which featured me? Indispensable. Throw away the empty whisky bottle — now that, yes definitely. Take the half-drunk cups of coffee back to the kitchen (I never drink tea, can't stand the stuff) and, instead of leaving them in the sink for three days, I set about washing them up. After an hour of this intensive activity which left me in a muck sweat, I looked hastily round my environment: you'd have thought it was a cottage in a Beatrix Potter story. All I had to do now was to go and sit back down on Mr Winterbottom's bench and smile.

★

I've always been perplexed by the complexities of when and when not to use the *tu* and the *vous* form in French. Not long after I'd come to live in France, I would find myself addressing the woman in the *boulangerie* as if she were the queen and talking to a policeman in the *tu* form which amounts to an insult. The way people scratched their necks and raised their eyebrows quickly led me to understand that I'd done something wrong, but it took a certain length of time and a certain number of conversations with both French and English friends for me to understand the subtleties and the mechanics of these two different forms of address.

Martine suggested that we should use the more relaxed and friendly *tu* form with each other, which represented a number of grammatical advantages from my point of view and which suggested, if I'd understood correctly, the possibility of increasing intimacy.

'Do you take sugar?' I asked, putting the tray down on a side table.

'Just a little.'

'Milk.'

'No, thanks,' she replied with a smile.

I'd thought of imitating the Queen Mother and having a separate teapot for myself full of gin, but I'd abandoned that idea pretty quickly. Any drunkenness on Her Majesty's part might be forgiven more readily than mine.

'It's a funny idea to come and live here on your own,' she said, looking round the room.

'Yes, it does seem to be.'

'Don't you get bored?'

'Sometimes, but you'd be amazed by how much goes on here.'

She raised her eyebrows as she brought her cup to her lips.

'Yes, yes, I know, it doesn't seem very . . . very . . . um . . . likely, but a lot goes on here.'

'It wasn't like that when I was here, when I was a child.'

'Did you come and play round here?'

'All the time. With my best friend. There was a place that really fascinated us.'

'Really?'

'Yes. Pisse-Chèvre. You must have heard of it.'

'Indeed I have.'

I outlined the various rumours I'd heard about my compatriot, although I omitted any description of the scene that I personally had witnessed.

'Perhaps it's because of the place itself.'

'What do you mean?'

'When I was little, an old man used to live there with his son. He didn't talk to anyone either. He hated everyone. He was called Isidore and, when the locals talked about Pisse-Chèvre, they called it "Chez Isidore". Except they pronounced it Ichidore.'

I remembered that there were lots of villages in, for example, the Limousin region whose names began with 'Chez' followed by a family name. Even the Malebranches did it, they used to take their sheep to graze in the garden of a ruined farm and they called it 'Chez Bertrand' in honour of the former owner.

'Poor Isidore, he was so thin. His wife had died. I don't even know what he lived off. You don't think about that sort of thing when you're little. He must have grown a few vegetables with his son.'

'Another cup of tea?'

'Yes, thank you.'

She'd taken her shoes off and curled herself up in the arm-chair, tucking her legs underneath her. Then she let her head drop back, resting on the back of the chair as she lost herself in her childhood memories.

'My friend Caroline and I used to take the little path from here and we'd go and watch him. It was very exciting, a real adventure. We dreamed up all sorts of horrible things that would happen to us if Isidore caught us. He seemed like an ogre to us. Poor man, he was harmless, really. So was his son. He's still alive, I think, I don't know what he does. I remember he left his father to go and work in Périgueux. Isidore was left all alone. And he was found alone, too, dead on his bed. He apparently had impressive amounts of alcohol in his blood-stream.'

'Tut, tut,' I said, wagging my head from side to side as if dev-astated at the thought of the tragedy meted out to drinkers.

At least Martine smoked a great deal, like many French-women, and she did it without any feelings of guilt, which was largely in her favour.

'Do you know the local doctor?'

'The new one? Apparently he's quite young and good-looking.'

'I wouldn't go that far.'

'No, I've heard him mentioned, but I've never met him. Why? Do you spend your whole life at the doctor's? Are you a bit of a hypochondriac?'

'Not at all,' I retorted, stiffening. 'It's just that he came here yesterday evening. He was chasing the old Dutchwoman's mad son.'

'Oh, the Weil daughter?'

'Do you know the story?'

'Of course I do, my great-uncle told it to us. The one who wrote the book. He was in a Resistance network during the war, too, and he hid quite of lot of *maquisards* in his church. Isn't it incredible, that story with the stinging nettles? After the war she married a Dutchman who wasn't in his first flush of youth. But he obviously wasn't really up to the mark because, according to the rumours, she stayed on very close terms with a childhood sweetheart, rather too close terms, even. He was her lover.'

'And is he still alive too? Does he live locally?'

'No, he doesn't live locally, but he owns the other half of your house. It's Jacques Duroc.'

I put my cup of tea down in sort of slow motion. Then I looked intently at her. I must have looked as if I were going to strangle her, judging by the air of anxiety that crept across her face.

'What's wrong, what's the matter?'

'Oh, nothing, nothing. But all these goings on . . . I just can't believe it.'

'What can't you believe about it? That's what life's like. Specially in a little village like this, not even a village, a hamlet.'

'Yes . . . yes . . . you're probably right. Possibly. But the mad son? Is he the Dutchman's son then?'

'You can't be sure of anything. A big boy like you should know that you can't ever be sure of anyone's paternity, short of doing tests, of course. But what's the point?'

That same question again, like the night before with the doctor: what was the point in saying that so-and-so had been murdered? What was the point in saying such-and-such's son was a bastard? I felt as if I were entertaining the concepts of a different era in front of these country folk who — along with their sense of 'what life's like' Martine put it — seemed to have adopted a tolerant attitude, which was still quite alien to me, towards things that I would have considered to be crimes, infidelities, betrayals and God knows what else. Just like the doctor, she contemplated all these issues with a profound indulgence that I would never have believed possible because I'd never met anything like it, except in books, and it seemed to me like an abstract problem whose only aim was to help steer some play towards a neater ending. But for these people, the people I was meeting, seeing, talking to . . . was it a form of forgiveness? The feeling that life punishes us enough as it is, without our needing to look any further, without telling the authorities so that they could set in motion processes that are usually indifferent to all the complications known only to the individuals concerned? Then the only possible answer to these questions came to mind: perhaps.

'Another cup of tea?'

'No, thanks, I'm fine.'

'Six o'clock already. Perhaps you'd like to have something a bit more . . . a bit more . . . grown-up to drink.'

'You mean alcohol? I'd love to.'

And this reply amazed me almost as much as her compassion for criminals and for adulterous women.

We had a drink and then another and I lit the fire, refusing her offer of help. Encouraged by the new heat from the drink and the fire, I asked her whether she had heard the Caminades' news.

'From down in the village there? Their son died quite recently, apparently. Poor things, they're all falling like flies.'

The comparison was a little brutal and I scratched my throat before going on.

'Um . . . I told you that the um . . . doctor was here last night.'

'Yes?'

'Well, he was saying that the last one, I mean the one that died most recently, was definitely murdered.'

She raised her eyebrows.

'The doctor came and told you that?'

'He didn't exactly come here with that intention, but I

invited him in, he seemed tired, he was obviously on his own, he needed to talk after a difficult evening and I actually brought him round to the subject. It was then that he told me, because, I want to make this clear, I brought him onto the subject, that there were signs of injuries on the body which suggested that he'd been killed.'

'Funny sort of doctor.'

I stifled an impatient response which might have led to regrettable consequences, but it struck me as extraordinary that she was more amazed by the doctor's confession than by the revelation within it.

'Yes, well, I don't know. But . . . um . . . it wasn't an accident.'

'What, definitely?'

'That's what the doctor thinks.'

'Even doctors can make mistakes.'

'But why would he have hidden the fact? He says it's so as not to make too much of a commotion. That's ridiculous.'

'Perhaps.'

Still the same response.

Then she added 'Perhaps he killed him.'

And she burst out laughing, before adding 'Hey, it is true that things happen in La Berthonie.'

It had been dark for a while now.

'Do you want to stay for supper?'

She hesitated, pursing her lips.

'Have you got anything to eat here?' she asked, as if it were highly unlikely.

And she was right. As she was finishing her question, I realised that all I had in the fridge was a half Camembert, a couple of eggs bought from the Malebranches a while back, a tub of olives, some rancid butter and a few other rare delicacies in the same vein.

'We could go to Brantôme in your car, but you'd have to drive me back afterwards.'

It looked like a trap, which of course it was. She knew that and she hesitated. Then, with a hint of a smile, she said 'Hmm, hmm,' which probably meant 'okay'.

7

It wasn't dawn, but you could be forgiven for thinking it was. The whole world was pale grey and the naked trees outside were painted in watercolour. There was mist everywhere and, even if the peasants were already up at this hour, there wasn't a sound, except for the sound that I alone heard of rustling sheets as Martine turned over in her sleep. You could still feel the last vestiges of heat given off by the stove, which would probably go out any minute. But it was still warm enough to give the illusion of comfort. I felt only a vague coolness under my bare feet.

That was when I saw her, scarcely disturbing the silence as she trod carefully. She hardly even made the occasional pebble roll on the path. I took a step back, because I sensed that she would look up at my window. I wasn't wrong. But she couldn't possibly have seen me, the room was in darkness. She paused very briefly, turned round and, like the last time, carried on slightly more quickly towards Pisse-Chèvre. Why did the old Dutchwoman keep going back to this dell guarded by a fierce dog and a mad Englishman? I couldn't reasonably wake Martine and pick up the thread of my rambling theories about murders. I decided to follow the old lady.

I gathered together my clothes which, in the heat of passion, had been strewn over the floor, on the armchair and around the bed. I was very quiet so as not to wake Martine and, without even bothering to put socks on, I tiptoed downstairs, carrying my shoes in my hand until I was outside.

The old Dutchwoman had obviously disappeared, but I knew the way. Cursing myself because I was lumbering around like a herd of wild boar, dislodging stones and twigs that rolled all the way down the slope, I finally arrived at the bottom of the hill on the edge of the clearing, near where the Englishman's daughter had been standing when I was on my way back from the funeral vigil. The old Dutchwoman wasn't there. Had she heard me coming? More than likely, so she would have hidden behind a tree until I'd gone past. Did she know she was being followed? She was certainly afraid of being followed. She hadn't been walking quickly enough to have reached Pisse-Chèvre. She must, then, have been going somewhere else.

There was a hut on the edge of the clearing, over the far side, at the top of the slope. Perhaps she'd taken refuge in there. I could just see one corner of the metal roof and the ancient piece of farm machinery rusting beside it, in front of a pile of logs covered with a tarpaulin so that they could dry out before they were brought indoors in the autumn. Then what? I really couldn't go straight over to these four walls of rotting wood, open the door and ask the old lady 'What are you doing here?'. It did occur to me, as I stood stock still and felt the dew soaking through to my feet, that I was like a child playing at finding bandits where there weren't any to be found, following people who'd led terrible lives, to accuse them of murders they hadn't committed. And yet there really had been a murder, I had the doctor's word on that. But it was hard to imagine the old Dutchwoman administering blows to the head of the colossus that I'd seen a few hours before his burial. There were other tracks, leaving the one to Pisse-Chèvre at right angles; it was perfectly possible, wasn't it, that the old Dutchwoman or the Weil girl or the Krug widow, had got into the habit of going for a walk in the mornings, taking the same route every day, in order to get away from her son for a moment, leaving him safely shut up in his room? And what if Martine woke up to find the bed empty? Was I going to explain that I'd surreptitiously followed one of my neighbours, because I suspected her of killing a woodcutter?

The February sun was breaking through the mist, the green of the fields seeped back as did the various nuances of brown in the mud; the trees in the distance etched themselves more clearly against the sky. I supposed I ought to get home quickly and pretend that I'd gone out to get some more logs for the stove, for example, or to buy some croissants. Definitely not, it doesn't take half an hour to go and fetch logs and you don't come back from the *boulangerie* empty-handed. Now that I was here, I might as well go and have a look in the hut which was only a hundred metres away. After all, I too had every right to go for a morning walk and to bump into the old lady quite by chance.

It was icy cold. I felt as if I were stranded on the flanks of the Himalayas and yet the bottom of the hill that led up to the forest wasn't particularly steep. With both hands, I held the lapels of my tweed jacket over my chest, irritated by my own stupidity, but it was as if a second person inside me, someone there was no reasoning with, was urging me on towards the hut which I was no longer looking at, so absorbed was I with the progress of my shoes through the long grass. From time to time I was aware of a beating of wings, which left me completely indifferent, but when I was only a few metres from the hut — five or six at the most — I looked up quickly when I heard a moan, a rasping sort of breath, followed by panting. I thought at first it was an animal and I turned towards the edge of the forest, panicking to think that I might have disturbed a wild boar or God alone knew what other fierce creature. But the noises, which had started up again, were coming from inside the hut. They were actually instantly recognisable, but so improbable in this setting that it took me a little while to identify them. I went over to the shed and walked round it and then put my face right up to one of the gaps in the wall. Inside, two bodies were wrapped round each other. I couldn't help feeling a degree of amusement at the idea that February nights in the Dordogne did seem to inspire intense passion. Was the old Dutchwoman carrying on an illicit affair with a young farm labourer who, judging by the evidence, was commendably vigorous? Had the man who owned half my house and who'd been her lover been living here in secret all this time? I glimpsed a young woman's face, which quickly invalidated my first hypothesis. It wasn't the Dutchwoman. I had to dredge through my memory to identify her, but there was no doubt about it.

The expression on her face at our first and only meeting had been very different from the one she wore now. It was the dead man's sister. Hanging on one of the walls of this smelly, godforsaken shack was the suit jacket and the carefully ironed, but cheap, shirt of the boyfriend who'd made such a scene in the middle of the funeral vigil. He'd kept his shoes and his trousers on and his trousers hung round his ankles. I couldn't tear myself away from this absurd spectacle. The crying and the sighs were starting up again and this time they were much higher-pitched than the roaring of a wild boar. Eventually, after a final groan, a final jolt of the hips, the young man rolled to one side with his eyes closed. When they'd both caught their breath, they exchanged all the usual declarations, as they lay on the beaten earth in the freezing cold. The man got to his feet, pulled his slightly shiny, pleated trousers back over his pink and white buttocks and tried to dust them down with his hands. A feeling of melancholy had all too quickly replaced the ecstasy and contentment.

'I'm fed up with doing this here, like this.'

'I know. So am I. But we haven't got any choice. Specially now.'

'We'll have to finish the job.'

'What do you mean?'

'They've all got to die.'

'Who?'

'You know very well who. It's because of your brothers that we can't see each other. And the old woman.'

'I won't let you talk like that! They are my family, after all!'

'If they were really your family, they'd care for you a bit more instead of stopping you doing what you want.'

'I've only got one brother left.'

'It's not much, but it's still one too many.'

'Stop it!'

She too had stood up now, she'd put her knickers back on and hooked up her bra strap. She was screaming at him, standing bolt upright with her arms held stiffly by her sides and her fists clenched.

'That was great and you always have to go and ruin everything!' she said.

'If you love me as much as you say you do, you'll just have to come and live with me in Nontron, or even in Périgueux, I dunno.'

'I can't leave now.'

'There's always a good excuse. It's like I said, the last one'll have to go the same way too.'

She buried her face in her hands and started to cry. He went over to her and she screamed 'Don't touch me! Leave me alone!'

I could tell that one of them was going to come out of the hut at any moment, probably the young man, and that I shouldn't hang about there. I was worried about her, though, I couldn't leave her alone in the middle of the forest, half naked, with a murderer who could strangle her with his bare hands for fear of her telling everyone he'd murdered her brother. At the same time, I was even more worried for my own safety. I had witnessed a confession. I backed away and I decided to take a longer route home so as to avoid crossing the expanse of the clearing.

I had momentarily forgotten about Martine and it felt as if

I'd been away for hours. In all the hurry, I hadn't taken my watch. After what I'd seen and heard, my heart was beating incredibly fast, it's appallingly banal, but there it was. I started to run through the forest, without worrying how much noise I made; after just a hundred metres it became apparent that I smoked too much, sweat was streaming down my back, my legs weighed a ton, and I felt as if the mud on the track was going to glue me to the ground. Then my strides fell into a rhythm and I saw myself on a rugby pitch, following my team-mates on one of those terrible days, exhausting days when you've gone to bed too late the night before and time drags out endlessly ahead of you, when you feel that the match will go on for ever, that you're always a couple of moves behind the action, a couple of moves behind the rest of the team and everyone's watching and getting impatient because you're useless. I skidded round each corner and twigs snapped under my feet. I turned round, it was absurd, to check that the young man wasn't chasing after me, a situation not without irony, considering I'd left the comfort of my bedroom to trail the old Dutchwoman like a suspicious boy scout. And I'd ended up finding the murderer making love in a shed on the edge of a wood. Seeing the rooftops of La Berthonie appearing, I felt as if I were arriving in another world, like waking up at the end of a bad dream.

I was still running as I arrived in front of the kitchen door. Martine was there, in my old dressing-gown, warming her hands round a big cup of coffee. She looked me up and down as I leant against the door frame, completely out of breath, my face streaming with sweat, no socks on and wearing just a T-shirt under my tweed jacket. She raised her eyebrows without saying a word.

★

'So you go for your morning jog in your tweed jacket?'
    'No, no, it's not that.'

'Then, were you playing detectives, by any chance?'

'Um . . .'

'Well?'

'Well, if I tell you, you won't believe me.'

'So romantic . . . do you want some coffee?'

'I . . . yes, I'd love some. Sorry.'

'It doesn't matter. Tell me your unbelievable story.'

I told her what I'd seen and heard that morning, trying to avoid too much detail to spare her blushes or perhaps my own, I don't really know any more. It was in vain, anyway.

'They were sleeping together in that hut?'

'Yes.'

'And you saw them?'

'Yes.'

'Why didn't you say so?'

'It's just . . .'

'Right, then. He was talking about "finishing the job". Come on, that doesn't mean anything.'

'But what about the rest? He wanted them all to "go the same way", as he called it.'

'It's not very sensitive of him to say it like that, but in the circumstances, it's understandable. Seeing they love each other.'

'Oh, very touching, yes.'

As she was probably right, I might as well be sarcastic. But I felt a niggling doubt all the same. More than a doubt, I wanted to have found the culprit in this whole business — which had nothing to do with me.

'And why would she have said "specially now"?'

'Because her brother's dead and . . .'

'Exactly!'

'No, no! For the sake of propriety, that's all. Her brother didn't like this guy. That's all there is to it. And these events are too recent for her to be running off and having a good time in her little shack. Bucolic but inappropriate.'

Even with her hair in a mess, her eyes puffy with sleep and standing naked under a man's dressing-gown, Martine managed to be half way between conventional respectability and a sort of independence which meant she could do what she wanted when she wanted.

'You know, you're beginning to worry me,' she said, 'with your stories of murder. It might turn out I've spent the night with a nutcase.'

'Perhaps . . .' I replied with a smile.

'But a pretty harmless nutcase, in my opinion,' she commented, taking another look at what I was wearing.

'You shouldn't judge by appearances.'

'First sensible words of the morning. You'd do as well to apply that rule to your inquiry.'

'Don't you think I should talk to the doctor about it?'

'About your mental state?'

'Stop it, please! I mean about what I've seen and heard.'

'I get the impression that you rather liked what you saw. There's always a risk that he'll have you locked up, I mean, why not? Is voyeurism punishable by law? I don't know,' she said, holding a conversation with herself. 'And, anyway, what about old Mrs Krug?'

'Yes?'

'Do you know what she was doing?'

'No, she disappeared.'

'Well, I never. You were given the slip by a little old lady. What a sleuth. Can I use the bathroom?'

Martine explained that she had to go and have lunch with an aunt or a second, or even third, cousin, the sort of relation you would never see in an English family. At first, I even thought it was an excuse. But she promised she'd be back and I preferred to trust her. She spoke in clipped little sentences, sounding more amused than annoyed. She could see that I didn't really believe her. I asked her when she thought she'd be back.

'Can't you wait to see me again?'

'Of course I can't.'

'This evening then.'

I couldn't help smiling. Especially as I wouldn't have long to wait before knowing whether she was lying or not. And I'd just had an idea which was going to make the waiting easier.

I hadn't been to pick up my new telephone directory, but things evolved sufficiently slowly in La Berthonie and the surrounding area for the information gathered under the covers of such a volume to be valid for at least five years, and in the old yellow pages left behind by the previous owner, I did indeed find the name and telephone number of the doctor who'd been to see me and had confided in me two days earlier.

8

Masses of women with masses of children were sitting on the chairs along the walls of the waiting room and, in the middle of the room, there was a low rattan table covered with old right-wing magazines. Every doctor in France has right-wing magazines in his waiting room whatever his voting preferences might be. A Communist newspaper in a Communist doctor's waiting room would be unthinkable. In amongst these magazines peopled by innumerable bespectacled men in grey suits, there were a few stray women's magazines with their population of models in sumptuous make-up, creatures only very distantly related to the women waiting there, who mostly wore pastel-coloured anoraks and trainers, looking ready for a long-distance run, but they too wore make-up because out in the country you always make a bit of an effort when you go to see the priest, the police or the doctor. Some were even wearing earrings, perhaps a sign that they were excited at the prospect of the GP's cold hands running over their bodies. Boredom in the countryside favours germs that are as damaging as the cold, the damp, the winter and the evenings that start too early. Nothing quite like feeling a stethoscope on your naked back for alleviating the monotony which is only usually broken up by unmentionable dramas. Even the children were cowed by the heavy, sombre atmosphere of this room, furnished so differently from every other room in the region: a kelim, a tastefully framed though rather neutral abstract print, antique furniture the like of which the patients' families had sold off long since to buy something more useful, only to regret the sale later when they saw the articles being displayed at outrageous prices in the smart antique shops in Périgueux, not to mention Bordeaux. They sat there with their hands crossed, their legs crossed and their arms crossed, almost hoping that something not too serious was actually wrong with them, serious enough to talk about it, but not to die of it.

Apart from myself, there was just one old peasant to represent the male sex. He was wearing clean blue overalls and he didn't know what to do with his hands which were crippled with arthritis. He wasn't reading and from time to time he lifted his bushy grey eyebrows to glance round at the others. He really was worried about his health, even if he was usually wrong.

Then the door opened and we heard a humble, grateful 'Thank you, doctor', then a few words from the doctor addressed to the child, more indulgent than those he spoke to the mother which were sometimes tainted with a hint of impatience. Out in the country, people don't hesitate before waking the doctor in the middle of the night because of a cold. Then the two figures, one small and one taller, would move away to the staircase which led down to the street. Then, with a glint of hope in her eyes, one of the patients (and never was that name more justified) would get up after her forty-five-minute wait and make her way to that chamber of secrets where such great things — life and death, good and evil, the future or the end of the world — were decided by a thermometer.

Then another person would come in from outside to replace the one who'd just disappeared out of sight through the door to the chamber. Sometimes the door would stand ajar long enough for us to see the doctor's silhouette and his regular features, the reassuringly square jaw and that impression he gave of thinking that nothing serious was really going to happen, not today.

It was then that he caught sight of me as I looked up from my right-wing magazine and I saw him quash a smile.

★

'So, are you suffering?' he asked me some fifty minutes later, still with the same twinkle in his eye.

'I . . . um . . .'

'You're suffering from an acute bout of curiosity. No need to take off your shirt for that, unless you'd like me to take your blood pressure anyway. There could be a link. You never know. Perhaps you'd like a prescription for some Vitamin C?'

'Perhaps. You know, you could at least acknowledge that it's not every day that people are called on by a doctor they've never met — when they're feeling perfectly well, too, as you've so rightly guessed — who then discloses that a murder has been committed near where they live.'

'You do realise that I've got patients waiting?'

'Yes. I've seen them. But they don't look any more ill than I am.'

He smiled again, but he lowered his head this time. A seventeenth-century drawing hung on the wall behind him, a blue and grey scene surrounded by folds and folds of draping. It was difficult to make out from where I was sitting and, anyway, had nothing to do with the practice of medicine.

'So, tell me, what intrigues you the most? The fact that I spoke to you about all this, the confession? Or the murder?'

'A bit of both, obviously.'

'I haven't got anything to drink here. I hope you'll forgive me.'

'What I really wanted to ask you was whether you have an idea who did it?'

'I don't give a damn.'

He looked me straight in the eye and there was a hint of

aggression in his expression as if he wanted to give me plenty of time to understand the implications of these words.

'It's their business. It's their problem. I said I didn't want to discuss it further last time I saw you.'

'And if I told you that I know who did it?'

I then saw a glimmer of curiosity in his eyes and for the first time I had a feeling — a rather satisfying feeling, I must admit — that he suddenly felt I'd beaten him at his own game. He leant forward without actually uncrossing his legs, but he nevertheless put his hands, which till then he'd held clasped under his chin, down on the desk. But, as he didn't want to shout out 'So, who is it?' straight away and as he knew that I would eventually reveal the murderer's identity, he found a way of delaying the revelation by asking 'And why are you coming to say this to me? Rather than to the police, for example?'

I hadn't been expecting this.

'Because . . . because . . . you were the first person to mention that it might have been a murder. And I think, rather as you do, that it's their business, after all.'

It had also crossed my mind that the French police would not necessarily lend a very willing ear to some foreigner telling them that one of their compatriots had murdered another of their compatriots and that I'd found this out by secretly watching two further compatriots of theirs copulating on the floor of an old shack. But I kept this thought to myself because I didn't know the extent of my doctor's nationalist susceptibilities.

We were like two chess players wondering which of us would resign himself first to losing a piece in order to move the game on.

'So? Who is it?'

There, he sacrificed his queen or his bishop. I hadn't been wasting my time. And incidentally, perhaps he too was finding that this consultation made a change from his usual fare.

I then gave him an account of what I'd seen and heard,

repeating what I'd told Martine word for word, but as he was a doctor I felt free to save myself any coyness and I included the details that I'd omitted for the latter's benefit.

Another silence, then 'Is that it?'

'Doesn't it seem enough to you?'

This time the smile gave way to a peal of laughter.

'It's too much even,' he said, finding it difficult to contain his mirth. 'And it's all the funnier because that wally you're talking about is my ex-wife's nephew.'

I probably went red enough to justify a consultation, then pale enough to require the same attention.

'Listen,' he said eventually, having regained something resembling his composure, 'I hope you had a good time watching what was going on inside this hut, but I can tell you that I think I know that young cretin well enough to be ninety-nine per cent sure that he's completely incapable of committing any sort of crime.'

'And the other one per cent?' I asked rather curtly, as if I'd been personally insulted.

'Even if he'd committed a crime in a rush of blood to the head, precisely because there's absolutely nothing in his head, he's far too stupid not to be caught or to try and cover anything up. All you heard was a lot of hot air. Not exactly tactful words, especially given the circumstances,' and here he burst out laughing again, 'but as far as anything else is concerned . . . That aside, would you like a prescription for some Vitamin C then?'

'But you yourself said that it was a murder.'

'Oh! Don't let's start all that again! Yes, that's what I told you and I'm beginning to regret it and, anyway, don't talk so loudly, I wouldn't want anyone to hear you in the waiting room. Doctors can get pathological about things, too, you know. It's a bit like when people tell their life story to a taxi driver or to a stranger on a train. Do you understand? What I said the other night still holds, but don't talk to anyone about it, okay?'

He managed to look impassive again as he made this last request and I got to my feet and headed for the door with my head lowered, just like the other patients, but certainly without their gratitude.

'I won't charge you for the consultation. Cures for boredom aren't funded by the state. But come again sometime and, as I said, I'd like to see your drawings. I prefer drawings to oil paintings. I don't know why, that's just the way it is. I always feel there's something a bit easy about oil painting, don't you think? I don't know. Right, on to the next! Ah, Madame Lespinasse! So, what's her boy got this time? Let's have a look at him, shall we?'

At least I'd managed to put him in a good mood for the rest of the day, despite the murder . . . which was still very real.

★

His ex-wife's nephew . . . wasn't that by way of being a confession? I had only a vague idea of the strong and complicated relationships within French families and I wondered whether his laughter wasn't actually a way of protecting himself or protecting someone else, just as he had protected whoever it was by refusing to reveal that a falling tree alone couldn't explain the death of a young peasant. It's not normal to laugh so readily about a murder, nor for so long, particularly after revealing the very existence of the murder during the course of a minor breakdown, or at least an unguarded moment. After all, he could have been obliquely confessing to the murder himself, lulled by the security of talking to a complete stranger. It was up to him — and him alone — to tell the police, who must have had their suspicions too, that the man had been beaten. They would have launched an inquiry which wouldn't have reached any conclusions and that would have been the end of it. But he didn't tell them. Why not? For the same reason that they all stood by each other and protected each other or that an old peasant who went into the Resistance as a teenager, knew that he had enemies who hadn't yet paid the price for their betrayals and denunciations. The roots of this murder or assassination ran deeper than those of the tree that had crushed the man I'd seen lying lifeless on his bed. I still didn't know why I was so consumed by curiosity about this affair, but I couldn't think of anything except finding the identity of the man who had beaten him to death and then made it look like an accident. And then there was the laughing doctor giving me half the enigma, implicating himself as he did so, sheltering behind his respected profession all the better to laugh. His ex-wife's nephew, now he had every reason to commit murder. The doctor had said it himself in my hearing, hadn't he? He'd said doctors could get pathological too. It was also conceivable that a man could hold sufficient affection for his ex-wife's nephew to hide his crimes.

There remained the question of Pisse-Chèvre. Unrelated, but still niggling at me. If the previous day had been more than satisfying, this day was proving to be full of frustrations. As Martine had said so concisely that very morning, I'd been 'given the slip by a little old lady'.

All these thoughts spun round my head as I rode home from the 'consultation' on my *mobylette*. It was only twenty past three. I had plenty of time to get home, leave the *mobylette* there and walk on down to Pisse-Chèvre to meet the antisocial Englishman. I mean, what could be more normal than for a sociable Englishman like myself to go and say hello and introduce himself to another expatriate, especially as I needn't have heard any of the rumours circulating about the man which, according to the Malebranches, were unfounded anyway?

The sound of someone playing the piano drifted over to me from the other side of the door. A sonata or something, I'm not an expert on classical music, an elegant tune, anyway, which was perfectly suited to the sense of isolation in the landscape. Melancholy notes which evoked for me the peaceful life of a cultivated family, dividing its time between reading by the fireside, music, perhaps a little painting . . . For a few moments the melody transported me to the Cotswolds, Bath perhaps, or to Kent, better still to Windermere in the Lake District, among green mist-hung hills, just like the ones around me now, but somewhere else. I remembered the Malebranches telling me that the Englishman's wife was a piano teacher. I hesitated before knocking on the door, because I didn't want to leave the England that this music had transported to me. I missed England and it was only now that I realised I did.

The door was pale green, the pile of plastic wine containers hadn't been moved and, standing in his pen a little way away, looking at me, was the billy-goat that the drunken, muddied Englishman had screamed at and threatened the only time I'd seen him, when his daughter was watching him. The house built in that crumbly local stone, the month of February, the forest all around me . . . none of it meant anything any more; that piano tune had somehow taken me back home. And, paradoxically, that feeling, with the help of the few minutes' pause, gave me the strength to knock on the door. The music stopped. Then nothing. I'd lost all notion of time just as quickly as my notion of space had become strange. Whoever was there, a woman — I was pretty sure — knew that I'd heard her playing the piano, she couldn't pretend that there was no one at home, she hesitated. I realised that she didn't feel like opening the door. Was it the Englishman's daughter or his wife playing like that? Despite the improbabilities of that moment, I knew the reaction that my knock on the door would elicit inside the house. Whichever one of them it was, she must know that people didn't like her family, they never had visitors, why would she want to open the door when she didn't know what hostile character might be waiting outside? Why couldn't people leave them in peace? They didn't ask anything of anyone and their lack of popularity surely stemmed from this desire to be left alone. And what was

I doing here, disturbing their calm existence? I knocked again, almost to apologise for disturbing them in the first place. I hadn't even entertained the thought that the drunken Englishman himself might be there, too.

I heard footsteps on a stone floor. A moment's wait and then the door opened.

Before even taking in her clothes and her appearance, I was struck by how well-spoken she was. It is a particularly English trait to be able to place someone both socially and geographically according to their accent.

'Yes?'

'I . . . um . . . I'm so sorry to disturb you . . .'

I don't know why she spoke to me in English straight away. My appearance perhaps? And I replied in the same language, hers and mine.

'Oh, not at all. Are you lost?'

She was holding the door half open with one hand, I could just see the Victorian pine dresser (*de rigueur* in English interiors in the Dordogne) displaying a selection of more or less valuable and more or less chipped plates. A kitchen table, also in pine, with a cup in the middle of it.

'No, I . . . I live in La Berthonie. I'm English and I've heard that you are, too . . .'

She looked me up and down, people are also judged on their clothes in England, like everywhere else, except the codes are a little different. She was wearing brown cords and a thick Norwegian sweater.

'It's kind of you to come and say hello,' she replied with a rather tense smile. 'We don't go out much, you know.'

We exchanged all sorts of banalities appropriate to English people in the Dordogne getting to know each other and we could quite easily have been in Windermere, Bath, Kent, I don't know, even Grantchester, for example. I caught sight of a brownish Barbour hanging on a peg on the wall, the one the daughter had been wearing the only time I'd seen her, perhaps they shared it. And what did it matter? She watched me without saying a thing, with a friendly smile, her cheeks reddened by the country air, but without saying a thing. There wasn't any more to say anyway. I couldn't ask her whether her daughter or her husband were there.

'I'm really sorry I can't ask you in,' she explained, 'everything's in such a mess.'

'I understand.'

This was all quite normal and that was what worried me. I had to face the fact that my behaviour had been absurd right from the start.

'Right then, goodbye.'

Then, just as I was leaving, she threw me a 'Pop in again sometime'. Foreigners are often caught out by this expression and they do sometimes actually go back, but by their very lack of precision ('sometime'), these words mean 'Whatever happens, don't get it into your head to come and see me again, because you're disturbing me and I don't like you, for these reasons which I won't speak out loud but which you nevertheless understand, I therefore hope that we'll never see each other again.'

I'd got the message.

The door closed as soon as I turned away and a few seconds later the piano tune started again.

9

Martine was in my kitchen when I arrived home; she'd decided to make the evening meal. She was standing in front of the cooker, stirring a wooden spatula round a big black cast-iron pan. She was wearing different clothes, but still as navy blue as before, with her hair tied back in a velvet ribbon, angelic, gentle, smiling, refined and slightly ironic, rather like a bourgeois version of one of Louis XIV's poisoners.

'What a charming domestic scene!'

'It is, isn't it? Have you been out hunting? Look, I've brought back a rabbit, I ran over it on the road.'

And she waved vaguely in the direction of an empty blood-stained rabbit skin which lay on the kitchen table. When I went over to pick it up, I saw the poor creature's severed head which eyed me balefully.

I retched and tried to disguise the fact, but it was pointless, she burst out laughing and asked me whether I was one of those Englishmen who didn't dare eat mushrooms for fear of being poisoned, who was disgusted by frogs' legs and snails and who was afraid of oysters. I replied in the negative to all of these questions except for the proverbial frogs' legs which I still hadn't actually seen anywhere. Martine then launched into a long diatribe on English cooking, a subject she obviously knew nothing about and I couldn't help thinking that this time she was the one doing a bit of export anthropology as she stood with one hand on her hip, waving her spatula, telling me about French cheeses, about all sorts of sauces which went with such-and-such a wine, about the great chefs, about how *recherché* this was and how delectable that was, and — still cooking all the while — she smoked one cigarette after another, letting her ash fall into the pan.

'Why don't we have a drink?' she suggested. 'I've brought some Pécharmant. Oh, by the way, I forgot to say, I dropped in on Sue on my way here . . .'

'Sue Brimmington-Smythe?'

'Well, yes! D'you know any others?'

'No.'

'Right, Sue then, and I asked her whether she'd like to come for supper this evening, I thought you wouldn't mind. Johnny was there, too, and that painter, what's his name again?'

'Thompson.'

'Yes, Thompson, so I asked them, too, because I'd run the rabbit over by then and I thought we'd have enough to eat.'

I was speechless for a moment.

'But will you be able to stay afterwards, when they've left?'

'Of course, why wouldn't I?'

In amongst the possible answers to this last question, I could have mentioned all the knowing smiles, the only slightly crude remarks and the downright crude remarks that I would have to suffer from my painting companions for months, nay even years to come, but I thought it better not to refer to all that at this precise moment, especially as the cork in the bottle of Pécharmant was putting up an unexpected amount of resistance. I was bright red, straining in every muscle and half crouching with the bottle between my thighs.

'When are they coming?' I asked with a belated 'pop!'

'It's amazing how people always ask that question and the answer's always the same: eight o'clock, eight thirty.'

I'd just have to keep quiet and fill the glasses, but I wasn't allowed to stay silent for long.

'You could ask me if my lunch went well, even though, I must admit, it couldn't have been more boring. And what about you, what've you been doing since I left?'

'Nothing much. I waited.'

'Waited for what?'

'For you, of course.'

'Of course. But when I arrived you weren't here. Who were you tracking down this time?'

'I went to Pisse-Chèvre.'

'Chez Isidore? What for?'

'Chez Isidore, if that's what you call it. To see the Englishman, but I met his wife instead. He wasn't there or at least I didn't see him. She didn't let me in. She was playing the piano when I got there. There wasn't any sign of the daughter either.'

'How disappointing! Is she pretty?'

'Oh, nothing special!'

'Oh well! And his wife?'

'Quite a large woman, seems very refined. Um . . . long . . . um . . . dark, greying hair, absolutely normal. That's the weirdest thing about it.'

'Were you expecting a witch with a hooked nose?'

'I was a bit. Because of all the stories about them. It's almost surprising that he's not a suspect.'

'Well, you never know . . . Mind you, I should think they tell enough stories about you, but that doesn't mean you're a suspect.'

'About me?'

'Of course, come off it! Of course they do! You're a foreigner, you're English, you live here alone, you don't work (in a place like this you couldn't realistically call your painting work), you don't have a wife or children, unlike your neighbour, and, also unlike your neighbour, you don't breed goats. If you were going to suspect anyone of murder, it would be you.'

'You underestimate the people here.'

'I'm from here.'

'Maybe, but I can assure you that I've never come across the slightest hint of xenophobia round here. Everyone's always been charming to me. No one resents or criticises the way I live.'

'That doesn't stop them wondering about it.'

'Most of them don't give a damn. They're far more tolerant than in London, for example, not to mention in an English country village like Grantchester. I was only thinking about that earlier.'

'And what made you think about it?'

'The Englishman's wife.'

'Her again! Anyway, you, me and the doctor are the only ones who know that it was a murder, seeing he hasn't told anyone else.'

'The family must have their suspicions.'

'Perhaps. But you can't be sure about that and, even if they did, why would they suspect the Englishman from Pisse-Chèvre?'

'Because he's unpopular. Or mad.'

'Half the community is unpopular, if you go by what the other half says. As for whoever committed this murder, he can't have been as mad as all that. He covered his tracks pretty efficiently anyway.'

She was talking as if it were something completely abstract, but listening to her I felt a shiver down my back, because I was beginning to register that all this had happened within five kilometres, no even less, maybe three kilometres, less than two miles away from my house.

'It's amazing how fascinated the English are with crime,' she commented thoughtfully, turning towards me with the expression of a perplexed explorer contemplating an ethnic specimen. Given that George Orwell had actually made the same observation before her, I didn't dare make a stand against so much authority in so many different forms: literary, female, English and French.

'Have another glass.'

'I'd love one. What else?'

'Nothing.'

'You didn't try to see the doctor again?'

My sigh served as a reply in the affirmative, an admission of defeat and a surrender to her greater powers.

'So, what was his diagnosis?'

'He took the mickey out of me and on top of that my assassin is his ex-wife's nephew.'

'He isn't!'

'He is.'

She broke into the same peals of laughter as the doctor and I had an uncomfortable feeling, on the one hand, that all of rural France was in league against me and, on the other hand, that they demonstrated a disquieting indifference towards a murder that had taken place under our very noses.

There were still two or two and a half hours before our guests would arrive and I made a few suggestions to Martine about how best to spend them.

'Impossible,' she replied. 'I've got to keep an eye on this casserole. You see, a wild rabbit has to simmer for a long time, normally you'd leave it to hang for twenty-four hours.'

'By the way, all this business about the murder . . .'

'Yes?'

'I'd be grateful if you didn't mention it to Sue and the others this evening. It wouldn't be a bad idea if we talked about something different ourselves for a bit and with them . . . well, you just don't know what they might make of it.'

'Yes, yes, I promise.'

★

'Did you know someone was murdered just near here?' Martine asked, practically shouting, when Sue, Johnny and Thompson had hardly got through the door and were just giving that traditional newcomer's glance towards the fireplace where four huge logs formed a roaring fire.

'They weren't!'

'They were.'

'How wonderful!' exclaimed Sue.

'Oh, my God,' said Thompson. And Johnny added 'Oh dear, oh dear, oh dear,' swinging his hips to left and right.

Then, nodding my head in greeting with a rather pinched smile, I concluded the subject with these few words 'But you mustn't tell anyone.'

Martine, who was behaving like the mistress of the house, told me to serve the drinks (which was absolutely pointless because our guests, in true English fashion, had already filled the glasses on the table with the various alcoholic beverages that they'd brought with them) while she went to deal with the rabbit she'd assassinated with her car and which she was cooking in some primitive way.

'So?' asked Sue, leaning forward in her chair. 'Give us some details. What happened?'

I'd hardly opened my mouth, re-crossed my legs, leant back into my chair, raised my glass and lit my cigarette when a woman's voice, Martine's, replied for me from behind me, talking over my head. She'd had time to turn over the jointed rabbit and come back.

Thompson looked unhappy because a man had lost his life and he disapproved of this demonstration of unhealthy interest in the subject; Johnny regretted that he couldn't establish a link between these events and his education at Bedales, his favourite subject of conversation (or should I say monologue) which came up at every meal like an indigestible pudding.

I found myself back in Grantchester. I'd never been to Grantchester so many times in one day as I did there, in the middle of the Dordogne, a stone's throw from Pisse-Chèvre and the Malebranches' manor house where they force-fed the ducks.

Martine told them about the doctor's strange visit to my house and about the rumours surrounding the Englishman from Pisse-Chèvre and, every time I wanted to add some detail or correct some small inaccuracy, she held her hand out to me and, without even looking at me, said 'Let me speak'.

On the other hand, Thompson, who was passionate about the French countryside, did manage to interject a little discourse on the origins of the name 'Pisse-Chèvre'.

It was then that Sue, who was smiling at the time, let out a terrible scream and brought her hands up to her face like a woman coming across a dead body in a film. She was looking straight in front of her with her eyes popping out of her head. Everyone stared at her until it occurred to us to follow her gaze. Simultaneously. And, again simultaneously, we all jumped at the sight of a face just outside the window. We must all have had the same feeling: that the man outside had been watching us for some time. We stayed absolutely motionless, not really knowing what to do, gripped with fear by this apparition which was both terrifying and comical and which produced a degree of embarrassment amongst the men at the table because no one wanted to be the first to get up and confront the intruder's distorted face. It looked like a mask, a bad joke. But he was very much there and he wasn't all that funny either. In the end, I got to my feet, not because I was the bravest, but for the rather ridiculous reason that I was the master of the house. My heart was hammering in my side and I'd already had enough to drink to make me unsteady on my feet. We'd been talking about murder all evening.

The man craning through the window, so that we could see only his face and his clenched hand, knocked again, more impatiently this time.

'He might be dangerous,' suggested Thompson, rather unhelpfully.

I opened the door and the man came over to me. He must have been about thirty, but it was difficult to put an age to him, which wasn't surprising given the state he was in. He had a strange ape-like posture with impressively wide shoulders, a short stooped neck and arms that seemed too long for him which swung beside his hunched body as he walked. He would probably have been taller than me if he'd been standing upright.

Then he looked up at my face and, foaming slightly as he spoke, he muttered in a hoarse, anxious voice 'He's dead, isn't he?'

It was obviously a question.

'I don't know. Who?'

'No, but he's dead,' he said again. 'You saw him.'

'I don't know who you're talking about.'

It was all quite absurd, but absolutely true.

'Have to go and tell them,' he said, raising an arm to indicate the darkness behind him as if it hid some important destination in its depths.

'Yes.'

'Have you told 'em?'

'No.'

'Have to tell 'em.'

I turned round as if to ask my guests what I should do next, they looked like wax figures frozen onto their chairs.

That was when I had a brilliant idea.

'Go and see the Malebranches. You do know the Malebranches?'

'The Malebranches?'

'Yes.'

'The Malebranches?'

'You must go and tell them.'

'Do they know he's dead? Because he's dead, isn't he?'

'Yes, yes, go over to the Malebranches, they'll know what to do.'

With flecks of foam on his lips, he turned on his heel and set off at a run, frenetically repeating to himself 'The Malebranches, the Malebranches . . .' until his voice disappeared into the night and I shut the door.

'That's Rachel's mad son,' announced Martine who was the first to grasp the situation.

A little later she told the story in its entirety, interrupted by frequent 'my Gods' and 'how horrible'. Johnny concluded that the mad son was the assassin and it was almost certainly the first time in his life that Johnny had pronounced a hypothesis that was within the realms of possibility, even probability. I myself was still pondering over the impressive strength that had emanated from that grotesque body. I'd read stories of demons with foaming mouths, they usually took place in, for example, Yorkshire in the nineteenth century, but this time it was by way of being on my home territory. No one would have believed me if I'd had to tell the story in London one day. I knew that the Malebranches would know how to deal with him with all the competence and patience of a psychiatrist in his white coat in a hospital, and this thought should have made me feel either per-plexed or full of admiration for them, but in the circumstances, I was quite unable to feel either of the above.

I went back to my place at the table and looked closely at my friends' faces. No one dared talk. I felt as if they wanted only one thing: to leave as soon as possible. Luckily, there was some wine left and we drank it. For the first time since his arrival in the Dordogne, Thompson agreed with Johnny and, giving weight to his argument with a broad spectrum of references, he explained why he was convinced that the madman had committed the murder.

Sue lit another cigarette and poured herself more wine, say-ing 'There's the bottle', even though everyone could see it quite clearly.

'No, no, no,' she said with a degree of assurance which gave the gathering a renewed sense of normality. 'A madman would never dream of covering up his crime like that.'

And she went on to develop the only theory she deemed possible about the murder, a perfectly absurd confabulation which implied the complicity of the entire village, the whole region even.

It must have been about half past two in the morning when I fell asleep in my chair, my ears humming to the vague echo of a few hesitant sentences from Johnny which were loosely related to the daily routine at Bedales when he was a pupil there.

After an indeterminate period of total but noisy darkness, I half opened my eyes to see a hillside of what looked like unusually bright yellow slugs, only to discover that it was the ashtray full of our cigarette stubs (Thompson, who was a vegetarian, didn't smoke). Then I felt something cold and round in my right hand and someone was pushing it up to my mouth. The bubbles travelling along my nasal passages indicated that it must be a glass of soluble aspirin.

A few moments later I found myself lying in a pitch black room that was spinning on its own axis and I heard Martine saying 'You poor old drunk, get some sleep!'

And that's what I did.

Thiviers in February is very like Scotland, it's as if the whole town could detach itself from the Dordogne, make its way to the sea and drift up to the East coast, somewhere just below Dundee. All the buildings look as if they're carved in granite, you almost wonder why you can't hear seagulls calling. The church looks greyer, the asphalt looks greyer, as do the few houses along the main street with their illegible plaques bearing the names of great men, now long forgotten, who came into the world or died in a dark room behind one or other of the grey façades. The windows shrink over curtains of synthetic white lace, everything turns to stone. And turns grey, of course. Until you forget the torpor of summer, the market days when you can wander slowly past the Dutch hippies selling royal jelly and beeswax candles or the English in their white tennis shorts worn slightly too tight over the buttocks and their sunhats that are just too small for their heads, who go on and on tasting the Bergerac wines, clicking their tongues and pretending to be experts.

It was market day and Martine had insisted that we get up early and go and buy anything that was edible and local, some of that Bergerac wine, for example, or some *foie gras* that hadn't been snapped up for the Christmas festivities and was still on offer.

The previous day had been given over to a slow and peaceful recovery from the night before, within the intimate surroundings of La Berthonie. Martine, therefore, felt that a morning's outing to Thiviers was essential. 'I'm from there myself,' she'd said by way of an explanation.

Johnny was there behind his bookstall, wearing his holey sweater and his affable smile, with a five-franc bottle of Bergerac standing open for all to see on the stall, rather more visible in fact than the leather-bound volumes of eighteenth- and nineteenth-century literature which, at this time of year, had no takers at all.

'God, this is awful!' he said, seeing us coming over, probably more in reference to the weather than to our presence or appearance.

He was wearing grey fingerless gloves like the peasant woman on the neighbouring stall whose vegetables were doubtless wonderfully fresh and full of flavour, but which just looked horribly muddy and sort of stunted.

'A swift one to warm you up?' asked Johnny, clapping his hands together and glancing round the swarm of navy blue anoraks shifting slowly around the square between the multicoloured awnings, which seemed to be turning grey in the cold, too, incidentally.

Behind Johnny, three old boys, always the same three, sat on a bench, sometimes leaning forwards onto a sturdy old walking stick, exactly like something you might see in a news report from a French village on the BBC.

The captain of the rugby team, something of a local personality, went past and threw us a cheery *bonjour* before going and saying hello to a Scottish architect — just right in this television scene — who played prop forward.

Martine and I felt, with varying degrees of sincerity and for a variety of reasons, that it would be preferable not to accept the drink Johnny was offering us.

'How's business?'

'Well, what does it look like? I'm really beginning to wonder why I come back every week. And I have to pay for the pitch. At least the wine's cheap.'

'Have you seen Sue again?'

'I went there last night, we had supper together.'

'And Thompson?'

'He wasn't there. Did you know he's doing some frescoes in a château?'

And Johnny burst out laughing as if that were the funniest joke he'd ever heard.

Every now and again he would raise one of his mittened hands to greet a fellow stallholder, a stout little peasant woman wearing a chunky sweater with a zip-up collar and a nylon apron, with calf-length boots and great thick socks on her feet. They responded to him with the same respect that Native Americans reserve for madmen, if Fenimore Cooper is to be believed.

It's always exciting setting off for the market; you always think you'll find unimaginable treasures, until you get there and realise that it's all the same stuff as the week before, that the fact that there are ducks' feet for sale doesn't justify the thirty-kilometre trip and that you still don't need French army combat trousers or a fishing rod.

It was at about that moment that the police van drew up outside one of the banks. Three men got out and went in through the glass doors.

Everything came to a standstill in the square. One policeman stayed outside on the door and made it clear to anyone who might want to go into the bank that they were not to pass him. A few moments later two other policeman came back out of the bank, each clasping an arm of the vigorous lover that I'd seen in full swing on the floor of the hut. The doctor's ex-nephew who was struggling and shouting 'I haven't done anything! I haven't done anything! She's lying, the bitch's lying.'

The only other sounds now were the distant rumblings of the odd car engine. The cold and the silence in the square acted like a wall around the action, echoing back the protests of the man in the threadbare black suit, tango-dancing in his attempts to break free from the patient and impassive policemen. He was pushed to the back of the van and the doors were closed. A moment later the van set off and within a few seconds, long enough for everyone's gaze to follow the vehicle's trajectory until it turned the corner and for their jaws to close again, the area under the awnings was filled with the excited hum of voices which follows any violent incident.

Martine looked at me anxiously as if I were hiding something serious from her. And Johnny let out a loud 'Oh!' and raised his eyebrows before pouring himself some more wine.

'Is it true then?' said Martine.

But I no longer had any feeling of satisfaction for having been right. This soap opera which had made the winter seem bearable was suddenly turning into a twenty-five-year prison sentence for a man in love.

We went into a café. I smelt that inimitable smell of a provincial French café, a mixture of dark tobacco, cold cigarette ash and pastis. The bar was half hidden behind four hunched backs in work overalls and topped with berets. Every now and then, one of the customers would swivel round on his elbow, which remained resolutely on the zinc top of the bar, to watch someone else come into the drab interior to buy all sorts of different lottery tickets, little bits of paper daubed in bright primary colours like plastic toys. Mind you, just by glancing out of the window over Thiviers in winter, anyone would have known that you couldn't possibly win millions on a game of chance here, not here.

The *patron* came over, his white hair combed and oiled back over his crown, a navy blue apron round his waist and a white cloth draped professionally over his left shoulder.

We ordered two cups of coffee, but I almost regretted refusing Johnny's glass of red wine. No one was talking. The four men standing at the bar kept nodding as if prostrating themselves in front of their *pastis* or their white wine. Their silent commentary on what had just happened.

'So you were right,' said Martine, warming her hands round her tiny cup of coffee.

And I replied with an 'It's awful' because it didn't really mean anything and I couldn't think of anything else to say. The fact that I had come so close to all the action after all, even down to hearing the assassin confess to the woman he loved, in almost comical circumstances, made me feel strangely uncomfortable, as if I had come too close to something which should have remained within the realms of fiction.

All voices sound the same in cafés and they all sound familiar, but when I heard the *bonjour* of the next person who came in, I couldn't help turning round.

'Oh, hello!' he said when he saw me.

It was the peasant with the Renault 4 that I'd met at the Malebranches' and who'd told me all about the old Dutchwoman.

Before I even had time to return his greeting, he'd set off on a sort of ritual welcome with the *patron* who was saying 'Ah, here's Marcel! So, not bringing us any good weather then!'

'Give me something to warm me up, can you?'

'The usual?'

'Yes, go on, the usual.'

'How's Jacqueline?'

'Oh, we're managing, we're managing.'

'Here, then, here's to you.'

Then he must have remembered that he'd seen me as he came in and he turned back round.

'So? What's going on in La Berthonie? Have you seen what they've gone and done? They've arrested him.'

'So he killed the um . . . the what's-their-names' son . . . Gaston, I mean?'

Martine seemed exasperated by my question and by the beginnings of this conversation, because she was born in a country which invented the *concierge* just so that everyone could have the pleasure of hating them. And at that precise moment she saw me in the role of *concierge*.

'Gaston? What do you mean? You mean his brother?'

'In the Renault 4?'

He gave a perplexed frown as if he were dealing with someone who wasn't quite all there or rather as if he'd suddenly realised that he hadn't ever met me after all and had been talking to the wrong person from the beginning. Doubtless out of courtesy, he decided to pursue the conversation all the same, while Martine watched me with an inverted smile, with the corners of her lips turned down to be precise.

'No, no, you haven't heard the latest. Yesterday evening, well, during the night really, the last Caminade son was killed. A knife straight through the heart. Didn't you know about it?'

'No.'

I spilt some of my coffee into the saucer.

'Yes, oh yes. And apparently it's the boy's girlfriend who got frightened. Even though she loves him, she went and told the police about him, because they say that he as good as said he'd kill her brother to her face.'

I already knew this, but I preferred not to tell him that, nor to explain how I came to know, because he wouldn't have believed me.

'How do you know?'

'One of my brother-in-law's cousins is a policeman and he told my wife earlier. We've got a stall a bit further up, opposite the post office, we sell a few vegetables. Seeing how little we make on it and how cold it is, I thought I was better off warming up in the café here,' and he threw a 'Hey, what do you say, Dédé?' to the *patron*.

'Oh, you know all about that, don't you? Never backwards in coming forwards where a drink's concerned, are you, Marcel?'

They could have gone on like that indefinitely, but I wanted to know more to feed and to calm my uneasiness at the same time. Just as I started to speak, Martine got up — rather abruptly, I thought — to go to the Ladies. Was that just an excuse to leave the table? Was it the cold that made her want to go? That particular mystery would be cleared up a little later and a little more easily.

'And how did he get in?'

'Oh, they never lock the doors over there. You know, out in the country . . . but they should. And here's the proof. But what shows that it was premeditated was the fact that the dogs didn't bark.'

'How does that prove anything?'

'They'd been poisoned, you see. Then he went in, he must have known there was no one there, he didn't make a sound going up the stairs and, you know, normally an old wooden staircase like that creaks.'

Even the *patron* was listening now, standing the far side of the bar with his arms crossed over his rounded belly, tilting his head slightly and raising just his right eyebrow.

'He went into the bedroom. Jean-Pierre, Gaston's brother, was sleeping in his grandmother's bedroom, and the little devil knew he was. He went straight there. Which proves that he knew their habits. He shook Jean-Pierre awake . . .'

Now even the policemen wouldn't have known that, but he was so enjoying telling the story that I didn't want to spoil it for him.

'. . . and just as the poor man opened his eyes, he sank his hunting knife into his heart. He must have been wearing gloves because he left it there.'

'Where?'

'Well, in Jean-Pierre's heart, for goodness' sake. And that's how the police found him.'

'And what about his grandmother? Didn't she hear anything? Did he kill her too?'

'Oh, her, poor old . . .'

Martine had come back from the Ladies and I was afraid that Marcel was going to launch into an indescribably violent account of what happened next. He took a chair, moved it up to our table and sat down before continuing. It didn't bode well.

'Poor old thing . . . No, he didn't kill her, but she must have seen everything, she must be over ninety, poor thing. I mean the grandmother, now, not the mother. Jean-Pierre was very close to his grandmother. He'd always been a bit frightened of his mother. A very domineering woman. She's a good strong woman, hard-working but, mark my words, she's not exactly a soft touch.'

'So, about the grandmother . . .'

'She went crazy. It was the shock, you see. It was like some nerve just snapped in her brain. She's hallucinating, foaming at the mouth, saying it was a ghost that killed Jean-Pierre, a ghost that talked to them in patois, mind you. As you can imagine, that young prat who works in the bank doesn't speak any patois. The young don't speak it any more now.'

I raised my eyebrows and nodded my head with a look of deep regret, even though in this particular incident the greatest tragedy might not be the disappearance of the local patois.

'They asked the old woman for a description of the murderer. But poor thing . . . she just went crazy. She just keeps saying that the devil killed her grandson. So you see . . .'

Then he turned to the bar and yelled 'Hey, can I have another one of these?'

And then he asked Martine 'And what would the young lady like? You shouldn't drink too much coffee, it's bad for your nerves. Especially if you drink it standing up, apparently. But you're all right here, we're sitting down.'

'No, I won't have anything, thank you,' replied Martine who'd listened to his story with growing interest, despite herself. 'Actually, we're going to have to go anyway,' she added.

'What's the hurry?'

'Oh, it's not that . . . but . . . I . . .'

'Come on, then. A coffee for the young lady.'

'Well, all right, in that case I'd prefer a glass of white wine,' she said.

I made the mistake of looking at my watch.

'Yes, yes, I know. It's a bit early to be drinking,' she grumbled before I'd even had time to make any sort of derogatory remark.

'And what if he's innocent?' I asked.

'What do you mean?'

'What if it was someone who really was talking patois?'

'When you kill a man in his bed in front of his grandmother, you're hardly likely to make a great speech,' interjected Martine, rather curtly I thought.

Marcel turned to her, nodding his head and wagging his finger towards her forehead as if to say 'Now there's someone who's sharper than you are.'

'Yes, but even so . . . by the time he's made a few threats and put the knife in . . .'

'Remember that there isn't any proof yet. But given that this is what the Caminade girl told the police, my brother-in-law's cousin said they were bound to re-open the inquiry into Gaston's death.'

The question that I'd asked a little earlier was not as stupid as all that then. Martine raised her eyebrows and flicked her eyes up to the heavens.

Another man came into the café and went over to the *tabac* till to buy a scratch-card which he rubbed with a one-franc piece.

'Well, well, there you go again!' Marcel called to him. 'You're at it again, René. I don't buy them myself, that way I win every week. Well, I'll be seeing you,' he said to us, getting to his feet and making for the bar because he must have remembered that René surely owed him a pastis or a glass of white wine.

'Right, shall we go then?' asked Martine.

'If you like.'

★

Everyone in the market place was talking frenetically and you could tell from the expressions on the anoraked stallholders' faces that it wasn't good for business, the customers were so pre-occupied they'd forgotten their shopping. But Martine, who had a passion for French cheese — so subtle, so varied and so many to choose from, so unlike the bland slabs of English cheese — asked endless questions of the cheesemonger from Bergerac who did indeed have all sorts of violent-smelling things for sale. Five minutes later I was really only half listening to this boring impenetrably Gallic exchange as I replayed in my mind's eye the scene that had taken place in the grandmother's bedroom: the hunting knife, the patois-speaking devil, a man murdered in his bed and a delirious old woman.

And it was then that I saw them. I would have recognised that silhouette in a thousand, the Englishman's daughter in her khaki-coloured Barbour, tall, thin, upright, walking beside her smaller, stouter mother, moving slowly like a pair of nuns or rather like English gentlewomen in an Indian bazaar, slightly amused by the picturesque disorder around them, aloof and, from their bearing alone, able to maintain the desired distance between themselves and the surrounding noisy, motley crowd who were probably not clean and certainly had some extraordinary habits. And yet, even the appearance of these memsahibs in the middle of Thiviers was almost normal, especially as their dark clothes — whose own cleanliness was not above suspicion

— in no way distinguished them from these people in their aprons and work clothes. In other ways, they did obviously look as if they'd come from Northern Europe and you could tell them apart from the locals, particularly because of their movements which were somehow both stiff and slow, languid almost, thanks to the boredom that they experienced every day and which they suffered in silence. Every now and then they exchanged a few words. I couldn't quite hear what they said, but you could tell by the way they moved their heads that there was a sort of cool courtesy in their intimacy that you would never expect between a French mother and daughter. Even England could surprise me now after the time I'd spent in France. Grantchester seemed quite exotic to me as I watched the way these two women walked. And yet that wasn't enough of an explanation. There were other English people at the market, Dutch, Germans, and they didn't look as if they didn't belong there. As if they didn't belong anywhere at all. And what were these two women who never showed their faces anywhere doing here in what amounted to a throng of people? No one threw them a cheerful *bonjour*. It was as if they were invisible.

Behind me I heard Martine saying 'So, two of those *crottins* and half a *reblochon*. The *camemberts* aren't too ripe, are they?'

Meanwhile, the man enumerated and suggested endless cheeses with increasingly ridiculous names.

That was when I took Martine by the wrist and almost shouted at her 'Come on, come on, back to the car. Come on, quickly. Look over there!'

'What? What's going on?'

'You see those two women?'

They'd just disappeared round a corner.

'Over there, come on quickly!'

I made her take a few steps to one side so that she could see round the corner of the granite house behind which the two Englishwomen had evaporated.

'Which women?'

'They've gone. It was the wife and daughter of the Englishman from Pisse-Chèvre.'

'So what?'

'So I want to go to Pisse-Chèvre while they're not there.'

'Why?'

'To see the Englishman. He'll be alone at the moment if he's there.'

'So what?'

'So it always comes down to the same people when there's a murder round Pisse-Chèvre. Don't you see?'

'No.'

'It doesn't matter. Hurry up.'

She paid for her cheeses with an embarrassed smile as if asking the salesman to bear with her for going shopping with her retarded older brother, then she bustled after me as I almost ran to reach the car as quickly as possible.

★

'Are you going to explain all this to me now, then?' she asked as we drove into Saint Jean de Côle.

'It always comes down to the same people when there's a murder.'

'You've already said that.'

'The old Dutchwoman the other day.'

'She's not Dutch.'

'Yes, yes, I know, I know, all right,' I replied, moderately annoyed. 'And that same evening, her mad son came and gaped at the window, foaming at the mouth like some monster.'

'Yes. So?'

'And that wally that they've just arrested.'

'You could show a bit more compassion. It was a crime of passion after all . . .'

'And now in Thiviers, the two Englishwomen from Pisse-

Chèvre and Marcel with his Renault 4, who — as if by chance — is the first to know what's going on.'

'I still don't understand.'

'Neither do I, to be honest.'

'So why are we trying to get to Pisse-Chèvre so quickly?'

'I just want to meet that Englishman. That's all.'

'I've had enough of all this. I'll wait back at your house, if it's all the same to you.'

*

The track that leads to Pisse-Chèvre is muddy and steep anyway, impassable for anything other than the ubiquitous Renault 4 or, for example, a Range Rover.

Without bothering to say a thing, I set off at a run down the hillside leaving Martine with the job of unloading the car and putting all the shopping away in the kitchen. Once I reached the bottom of the hill I stopped to catch my breath, impatient to get on and meet, on friendly terms if possible, this bear from Pisse-Chèvre whom no one but the Malebranches liked and who was the only person left in the community that I hadn't properly met, unless you count the day when I saw him blind drunk, wallowing in his billy-goat's droppings.

I paused for a while as the house appeared round a bend in the track. The billy-goat was still there, and it watched me with a mixture of disdain and indifference as it tirelessly scooped its bottom jaw from left to right. The wind was moaning through the trees. The Englishman's things, his tools and his cars, were scattered around outside the house as if he'd just abandoned them there half way through some job and would one day pick them up again to complete the task which had, in all probability, been interrupted by his state of inebriation.

Within a few minutes I'd managed to convince myself that I wasn't, after all, spying on anyone, but that I was just calling on a neighbour. I carried on with more determination and then saw that the door was open. This was better than I'd hoped for, because now he couldn't pretend he wasn't there if I knocked on the door. Before I even reached the doorstep, I heard a woman's voice, a well-spoken voice which nevertheless had a ring of anxiety in it as it asked in perfect French: 'Is that you?'

When I reached the threshold I saw that there was someone sitting at the table with her head in her hands, it was the old Dutchwoman, Rachel, motionless, waiting for someone. I no longer knew what to do or say next. I couldn't possibly go in or even retrace my steps without being seen. She looked up and then, recognising me or rather realising that she was looking at a stranger, she started. Her face was bathed in tears. She said nothing, but just looked at me with wide, staring eyes. Then she stood up, knocking the chair over behind her, brushed past me and ran off up the path towards the château like a mad woman.

I hadn't stammered out a single word as I watched this old woman stumbling and waving her arms around dementedly as she ran off through the trees. I felt as if my lungs were filling with ice. I didn't even know which word to use to describe what I'd just done by turning up there: was it indiscreet, criminal, ill-mannered, a mistake, a blunder? Whatever fault I had committed, it was irreparable. You don't happen across an old lady in tears in a stranger's house just out of curiosity.

*

Martine was sitting in the kitchen with Madame Malebranche, drinking another cup of coffee and they watched me arrive with my head lowered, my face either flushed or pallid with shame, I'm not sure which, there was no mirror above the cooker.

'What's happened to you?' asked old mother Malebranche. 'You look as if you've caught a chill.'

'I may well have done.'

'I came by to say hello. It's been a while since you came to see us.'

I didn't have much to say in reply, so she said something for me.

'You must have been busy,' she said with a chuckle, probably with reference to Martine's presence.

I couldn't help smiling myself, because I would never have suspected that old mother Malebranche was capable of the even most subtly suggestive remark.

'I came and had a chat about what's been going on with your ... your ...'

She didn't know whether she should say your lady friend, your wife or your sweetheart and she was going to leave it hanging in the air when the interested party herself came to her rescue.

'Martine,' she said.

'Yes, Martine,' repeated old mother Malebranche.

'Have you heard?'

'The latest murder.'

She raised her arthritic hand and let it fall back down onto her thigh, then swinging her entire body backwards and forwards like an orthodox Jew at the Wailing Wall, she added 'What sort of luck is that!'

I was about to rejoin with a 'Tch, it's the very devil,' but I curbed myself at the last moment.

'Oh, well,' she said, 'at least it wasn't the young man they arrested.'

'What do you mean?'

'Well, yes, they took him to the police station, Jocelyne told me you saw the arrest."

'Martine,' Martine corrected.

'Yes, Martine. But in the end it's not him. Poor boy, he was in such a panic, he couldn't even speak. But he was out dancing on the night of the murder.'

'In a nightclub,' explained Martine, who found this description of the Manhattan at Brantôme somewhat off the mark.

'And as he was in a bit of a state ... he'd been drinking, you know ... some friends brought him home in a car at about five o'clock in the morning. So he had a lullaby, as they say.'

'An alibi,' corrected Martine who seemed to be in an extremely good mood.

'Yes, like you said.'

'And how did you find all this out so soon?'

'From the postman. He's a cousin of mine and, when he brought the post, he told us everything because his sister-in-law ...'

I didn't actually hear the rest because I was sighing so loudly.

'Tch, well, you'll have to come up and see us one of these days with ... with ...'

'Martine,' Martine repeated again.

'Yes, like you said.'

'All right then, byebye ...'

And she shuffled off, still muttering all sorts of 'tchs' and 'Well, I nevers' and 'Well, there you ares'.

$$11$$

'Do you know what I saw in Pisse-Chèvre?'

Martine wasn't interested, she had much more important things to tell me.

'Sit down,' she said.

This was a bad sign, yet another on a day that should have started so well and which came on the heels of an almost perfect day, etc.

I thought for a fleeting moment that she was going to give me the name of the murderer or the key to the whole saga. Not at all.

'I have to tell you,' she began, 'that I've got to leave, you see, it's the end of the February holiday.'

I felt all the icy chill associated with that particular month of the year when I thought of our imminent geographical separation.

'Couldn't you stay on a bit longer?'

'I really couldn't. And there's something you should know. I really like you but . . . um . . .'

Definitely not a good sign.

'Yes?'

'I don't think we'll be able to see each other again.'

'Oh? But . . .'

'No, come on, let me speak.'

And then she didn't say anything.

'Bordeaux's not all that far, I could . . .'

'No, no, no, no . . . Listen!'

'Yes, I'm listening.'

'You see, I've got a boyfriend in Bordeaux. We've been going out for four . . . no, five years and I really like him. I really like you too, but, well, I was on holiday and . . .'

'Oh . . . But . . . Even so . . .'

'Please, it would be ridiculous for us to have a scene, everything was so good up till now. That's just life, you see.'

'I see.'

'Are you angry with me?'

People never say yes when they're asked this and they're wrong not to.

'And when are you leaving?'

'Tomorrow morning. But as tonight is my last night here, I'm going to stay with my aunt.'

Our goodbyes were rather formal, almost solemn, and three minutes later, after hearing the sound of a car engine and watching a car disappear round the corner of an old farm building, I looked at the second armchair by the fire. It was empty again, but instead of the redhead I had dreamed up it was occupied by the memory of Martine.

★

Every sound reverberated around the house, my softest footstep on the tiled floor; the tinkle of the bottle against the glass, of course, but it sounded like a cathedral bell; the logs crumbling over the glowing embers in the fireplace after burning for hours. All sorts of reminders, souvenirs of Martine and her absence, were dotted about the various rooms: the glass she'd drunk out of which was still half full, the wood that she'd made me bring in and stack by the chimney so that the fire didn't go out; she'd even left a pair of tights in the bedroom, next to the unmade bed.

At about half past seven, I heard someone knocking on the

door, three sharp little knocks. I jumped to my feet and a huge smile must have spread over my face: it was Martine, she must have changed her mind, she'd decided not to go back to Bordeaux, to drop the boring bloke she'd been seeing there, she was giving up her law studies to come and paint watercolours between Pisse-Chèvre and La Berthonie.

I opened the door: it was the old Dutchwoman in a woollen bonnet, a grey wool skirt and an anorak, she was wearing thick navy blue tights, also in wool, and sturdy shoes. She looked like a cultivated old authoress who liked to take a walk in the countryside, all she needed was the shawl.

I stared at her open-mouthed, not knowing what to say. Her face was both distinguished and severe; her eyes were pale, washed-out, but they looked the world squarely in the eye with a glint of determination. I noticed that she was wearing make-up, face powder and pink lipstick, which struck me as rather surprising for a widow who lived on her own in this part of the world.

'Am I disturbing you?'

'No, not at all, please come in.'

'It's just I haven't much time.'

'Come in, anyway. Sit down.'

'No, thank you for offering, but I won't sit down.'

I thought she was going to tell me to stop following her, to mind my own business, that she'd been living there for long enough without some newcomer coming and spying on her at every opportunity.

'You must have thought me very rude this morning,' she said, 'when I saw you at Piche-Chèvre.'

I was more astonished by her pronunciation of that name than by her words.

'But, you see,' she went on, 'I was looking for my son. You must have heard people talking about him, perhaps you've seen him?'

'Um . . . I have, the other day, he was hanging around here. He came and knocked on the window.'

She looked horrified.

'Oh, my God, I'm so sorry. But he's harmless, you know, he wouldn't hurt a fly.'

'Are you sure you won't sit down, would you like a drink?'

'No, thank you.'

'A cup of tea perhaps?'

'No, really. I don't know how much truth there might have been in the stories you've been told, but it's very difficult for a woman like me, of my age, to look after her son on her own, do you understand?'

'Yes, of course.'

It was not so easy to understand why she hadn't sought medical help or something more along those lines.

'What frightens me most is the thought that he might hurt himself, it's him I'm worried about, you see, because he really is harmless.'

I thought she was protesting a little too much. Could it be that she was trying to cover up her son's guilt? Was Sue wrong in believing that a madman would be incapable of covering his tracks after a murder? And what was the extent of his madness? But I couldn't exactly ask his own mother.

'And when you found me so upset "Chez Ichidore", it was because I couldn't find Louis anywhere. Louis is my son. He often heads off in this direction, you see.'

'Towards Ichidore's.'

She looked up with a smile.

'Yes, I mean Piche-Chèvre, or Pisse-Chèvre, it's what we used to call the place, after the old man who lived there.'

'Yes. I know.'

'Right. Oh, listen, I'm terribly sorry to have disturbed you.'

'Not at all.'

'But I have. I won't stay and keep you from your work.'

She must have seen and known perfectly well that I had nothing to do and on that particular evening I would have been grateful for anyone's company. But she turned on her heel and disappeared off towards her château.

It was only after she'd actually left that I managed, with great difficulty, to establish the link between this polite, upright old woman struggling with her terrible burden of responsibility, with everything else that I knew about her. She was the naked young girl whose mother had whipped her with stinging nettles. She had been the mistress of my neighbour who'd disappeared off the face of the earth, and the wife of the Dutchman who'd survived one of the concentration camps. The Weil girl. The Krug widow. The Dutchwoman whose walls were hung with the sixteenth- and seventeenth-century *danses macabres* that her husband collected. I tried to imagine her when she reached the château, going across the gardens and opening a massive wooden door into a hall decorated with obscene, macabre, black and white images.

But very soon my thoughts went back to Martine. I couldn't help smiling, albeit rather bitterly, as I realised that what she'd done and the way in which she'd done it ('Don't be angry, darling, but I've got another man somewhere else and I love him very much, etc., etc.') corresponded exactly with the clichéd image that the English have of the French.

I hadn't bought any whisky because I'd begun to believe in the future and in any case we'd left the market in too much of a hurry, again my mistake, to fill up with the Bergerac at five francs a litre. I was onto my fourth cup of coffee and my fifteenth cigarette of the evening and my hands were beginning to shake. At my age that was worrying. Actually, at my age, everything around me was completely absurd and, as the evening wore on, I came to the conclusion that it would all have been more than worrying at any age. An open fire, an empty room, not a drop of whisky to be had, no chance of going anywhere else or doing anything other than sitting watching the flames consuming the wood, producing a negligible glow of heat from which I didn't dare stray. And night still fell too early and the armchair opposite me was still empty and Martine still hadn't turned her little car round to come and tell me that she'd changed her mind.

Then my thoughts went back to the old Dutchwoman as she climbed the monumental staircase leading up to her bedroom. She would pass by the locked door to the room in which her mad son was cloistered. The shutters would be firmly closed too. She might listen at the door, to be sure that he hadn't escaped, perhaps she would be reassured by the sound of his steady breathing, as I hear the wind outside reminding me that the world still exists and that I'm like an old widow myself, waiting for time to pass. I could ring up some friends, get them to ask me over, drink their wine. I haven't even the strength to pick up the telephone and I'm not going to stoop so low as to play the role of the deserted lover and to ask for their shoulders to cry on. I get up out of the armchair and take a few strides across the room. Perhaps the old Dutchwoman is pacing round her bedroom, a room in which she's never felt happy. I wonder whether she keeps her château tidy, I would have thought so, judging by that air of melancholy that she carries with her everywhere she goes, from her slow footsteps and her clean clothes, shapeless but still somehow elegant, or at least adequate. My house isn't going to stay tidy for long, that's for sure. What's the point, anyway?

I start making plans: I must leave this place, sell the house. How much should I ask for it? I'll get less than I paid. It's only a semi.

I get up, go back to the kitchen and go into the utility area which the locals call the cellar, but it isn't a cellar at all because it isn't underground. The house doesn't have any foundations, the men who decided to build it just piled stones on top of each other, some areas of wall are even drystone and in places, where the balcony is, for example, limestone has been put over the drystone wall to make it look more noble and elegant. I start ferreting around looking for a bottle that I might have forgotten there. It's pathetic, but no one can see me. I get a spider's web caught on my hair and I can vaguely hear a scratching sound, a sort of frenetic and furtive movement. Rats. That's all I need. Perhaps it's only a mouse, but that's bad enough. I need a cat. No, actually, that's the last thing I need. A bottle of Cahors . . . empty . . . another bottle of Cahors, also empty. Five plastic containers of the Bergerac at five francs a litre, no hint of a liquidy noise when I shake them. Two bottles of Laphroaig. More than empty. I drink too much. I'll have to cut down my intake starting from tomorrow, in the meantime, there really must be something . . . I come across my Cambridge gown hanging on a nail, its shoulders grey with dust. On the shelves I see a book that I looked for frantically barely three weeks ago. Cardboard boxes left over from when I moved here and which I still haven't opened after two years, a pair of gumboots and a deflated rugby ball. I remember a bottle of Château Pavie, empty . . . Two bottles of champagne — it has to be said: the bottle bank is far too far away. And the dustbin men leave the bags by the side of the road if they hear the tiniest tinkle of glass. Some gardening tools, perfectly charming things whose only use now is to provide a home for whole armies of spiders. A rusty screwdriver barely a foot away from the toolbox, which goes to show that some degree of order has been respected. Three broken glasses on the shelves. A pack of cards . . . why don't I start playing bridge? With so many English people in the area, there must be an English-speaking bridge club.

In the end I find a muscatel, sweeter than candyfloss and the tacky consistency of poison, but it certainly lives up to its fifteen degrees. A couple of friends, Anne and Mark, entrusted it to me before going back to England where Mark had got a new job. We'd become friends and I used to see them quite often, but after a year they headed home with their daughters. They told me that the young man who was moving into their house to keep an eye on it while they were away was a drunkard and it was best not to leave any bottles within his reach. Wise decision. Then suddenly everything seems to come right because on top of the wooden shelving unit I catch sight of the conserves that I made myself, shortly after my arrival, in empty Nescafé pots: plums, blackberries, raspberries and cherries marinating for the last twenty-four months in eau-de-vie, but I had added rather too much sugar to it, producing an extremely strong and perfectly noisome concoction. So I opt for the muscatel.

The neck of the bottle feels sticky, so does the red plastic cork and, on further inspection, so does the sort of Italian plaited basketwork round the bottle. I find a cheap old mustard glass in the cupboard, it smells of dust and damp — it is as suited to my muscatel as a flute is to champagne — and I half fill it. I take it back over to the fire, no longer feeling so sorry for myself, and I light a cigarette as I begin to regret that the old Dutchwoman . . . the old Dutchwoman . . . it's amazing how I've adapted to life here, even knowing perfectly well that she isn't Dutch, I've started referring to her as that . . . what was it I was regretting? Oh yes, that the old Dutchwoman hadn't stayed and had a drink, or two even, I'm sure that the muscatel wouldn't have frightened her off. And it strikes me that, at the end of the day, I've got more in common with the old Dutchwoman than anyone else in La Berthonie; we're both almost foreigners and almost not, we're both alone and would surely prefer not to be, I don't have a mad son, but I'm going to become one if I stay here another six months. I really should have said yes when Martine asked whether I was angry with her. And what if *she*'d killed them all before escaping back to Bordeaux under a false pretext? There, that wouldn't surprise me!

All of a sudden, I wondered why the Dutchwoman came to explain things to me. Why had she suddenly felt the need to explain what she'd been doing in Pisse-Chèvre? Especially as her story didn't hold water. She may well have been chasing after her son again, granted. But then why hadn't she called the doctor out again? So as not to disturb him, she couldn't call on him every time. Yes, at night it was understandable, but on a Saturday morning, when the doctor's off-duty . . . Still, none of that explained why she'd been inside the house. It's true that out in the country they don't lock their houses, or rarely. But that doesn't exactly mean that you can just go into anyone's house and cry your eyes out whenever the fancy takes you. Which all goes to prove that there was some connection between her and the Englishman from Pisse-Chèvre. But how close a connection? (The muscatel was frankly undrinkable, but I poured myself a second glass, persuading myself that it would help me sleep.) Anyway, there was nothing to stop her granting this man the same indulgence — friendliness even — that the Malebranches felt for him. She herself was the subject of so much gossip that she'd had ample opportunity to take everything that people said and thought with a large pinch of salt, especially as she was cut off from the rest of the community. And what relationship was there between the Englishman's wife or daughter and this false Dutchwoman? Had the Englishman been hiding while she sat there crying and his wife and daughter were out at the market? And what about what she'd said? 'Is that you?' in French. Perhaps she didn't speak English. Perhaps she thought it was her son coming up to the open doorway.

Hardly important to me this evening compared to Martine's absence on the one hand and the presence of the muscatel on the other hand. Their combined effect managed to make me feel nauseous.

A rat again. A scratching sound, further away than the one I'd heard in the cellar. The noise was actually coming from above me. Rats rarely live high up, they prefer cellars and holes in the ground. Perhaps it was a bird taking refuge in the attic or a ferret. No, a ferret would have made more noise, it would have knocked things over, forcing its way through planks of wood like a pneumatic drill. I'd seen the damage they could cause in a friend's house, a far cry from this steady, regular scratching sound. I went up to the bedroom to look at the ceiling, because I didn't dare go up into the attic. And the ceiling didn't give me any clues, obviously.

On the other hand, I could still hear the noise, like a cat sharpening its claws on a very old and very valuable piece of wooden furniture. The house is built in such a way that, to get to the attic, you have to go through my studio across the landing from the bedroom, pick your way between the palettes and the sketches all over the floor, go through a door on the far side of the room and come out onto the stone balcony. From there a rope-ladder leads up to the attic where there is no electric light, so I had only the incandescent end of my cigarette and the flame on my little lighter to guide me. My footsteps reverberated through the rotting floorboards as if an entire army were inspecting the place. But oddly enough, since I'd climbed up the rope-ladder, the scratching noises had stopped. When I realised this, I managed to carry on in silence, by walking on tiptoe. As the lighter warmed up it burned my fingers, but my eyes were gradually becoming accustomed to the dark. A few beams of moonlight filtered through the little square gaps that had been left in the ancient stone wall, picking out the stones and the wood with a greyish light. The wood creaked. From time to time a bat would leave its perch with a flutter of wings, making me jump and then cover my head with my hands because I still believed that bats could get caught up in your hair. I'd finished my cigarette and ground it under my shoe. I was short of breath, anyway, so I'd almost forgotten I was smoking and my heart was beating too fast. Suddenly I saw myself there, as I must look, hunched in the darkness, frightened, looking about me nervously in an attic that was manifestly empty, my stomach tortured by the muscatel . . . and I almost burst out laughing, only the scratching then started again. This time it was accompanied by laboured breathing, a sort of whistling sound. I turned back, the noises were coming from the other half of the house, in the exact spot where a door had been walled up between the two halves of the attic.

I stood there, petrified, unable even to think. I tried to swallow but my every movement was unconscious and quite independent of my will. I think that I ceased to exist the moment I understood where the noise was coming from. I was frightened.

Then I hurried back down the ladder, ran right through the house and went outside to try and inspect the other half of the building. I ran round the whole thing, gazing up at the sky. I waited before going back into my half, but even there, I no longer felt safe.

There were just a few embers left in the fireplace. I lit another cigarette with a hand that shook so much that the tobacco and alcohol alone couldn't have been responsible. I sat in the armchair, but didn't stretch out and relax, I had all the apprehensive tension of a soldier the night before battle. As if the devil were about to come and kill me, cursing me in patois. Every now and then, I would throw a sideways glance at the metal rod that I used for stoking the fire, thinking that I could always defend myself with that. It was obviously out of the question to go to bed.

And yet, I couldn't call for help either, certainly not from the police, because it might be nothing when all was said and done. Just a rat. After all. It was this final objection which allowed me to think logically and to come up with all sorts of hypotheses, none of them very reassuring, but at least I could think again.

The first hypothesis was that the Dutchwoman's mad son had broken into the house. He'd killed them all and he was in there inflicting God only knew what sort of torture on himself behind these ancient stones, as he tried to scratch off the mortar with his bare hands . . . And when the Dutchwoman came by earlier, it was because she was looking for him. But then why would she have knocked at my door? The second hypothesis was that the murderer was there and he'd chosen me as his next victim. But why? It didn't make any sense. In either instance, how would he have got into the attic? By climbing up the front of the house and slipping in through one of the skylights. Possibly. But that would have required a rare degree of athleticism. A madman would have been capable of it, though.

The third hypothesis (which was really only the first one) kept coming back: I was the victim of my own imagination. I'd heard some animal, a rodent or a bird.

12

The Malebranches couldn't help laughing when I told them my story. And yet . . . for all their laughing and their nodding of heads, I thought I detected a quick glance between the mother and the son, furrowed brows, a pursed mouth that suddenly tensed. It could be that I dreamed that up. As well as everything else. Perhaps I only thought I'd glimpsed what I wanted to see.

I'd woken half an hour earlier, still sitting in the chair where I'd succumbed to sleep and to the muscatel despite commendable efforts to resist them both.

'A white lady,' explained old man Malebranche.

I thought they were going to subject me to some old superstition, doubtless a very picturesque one, but in the circumstances I wasn't in the mood to appreciate Périgordian folklore.

'A . . . um . . . white lady?'

'A bird. You know.'

'No, I don't know.'

'Barn owls, we call them that because they're all white.'

'They're a protected species,' added the son, introducing a more scientific note.

'Are there not many of them left?'

'People used to kill them because they brought bad luck. They used to nail them to barn doors.'

Exactly the sort of barbaric and Continental custom which would have both thrilled and disgusted the BBC, I could already imagine the hours of Radio 4 broadcasting dedicated to the subject and the listeners asking what the European Commission was doing to ban it.

'Did they nail them up alive?'

'If they could, but the wretched things struggled so much, they usually killed them first.'

'Your mother did that once, didn't she, on that barn there? D'you remember?' asked old mother Malebranche to refresh her husband's memory and darken her mother-in-law's name in one go.

He shrugged one shoulder in resignation.

'Poor woman, she didn't know any better.'

He tried rather clumsily to give us some explanations which would have required using the word 'superstition', but the difficulties he had pronouncing the word eventually persuaded him against it.

I myself looked over towards the barn in question, almost expecting to see the Gothic spectacle of a round-eyed, white-winged bird hanging there, dripping with blood, scarlet against the faded green planks of the door.

'And did they stay there to rot?'

'Well, when they smelt too much, they'd be taken down,' she replied, speaking wearily and weightily as if she were being forced to accumulate evidence for someone who was rather slow in grasping the point.

'If you wait, you'll see her leaving this evening.'

'Who?'

'The white lady. Sometimes they live in pairs.'

'Really?'

'Yes, you hear them calling, like this . . .'

Under my very eyes, old mother Malebranche transformed herself into an old bird, she curled back her lips to expose what few teeth were left to her, yellowed triangles planted at angles in pale pink gums, then she produced a long, high-pitched and menacing-sounding cry, the sort of noise that an axe would make bearing down on the neck of a condemned man in the Tower of London. But longer, not so cutting, if I can use that word, almost melancholy but still sinister.

'They don't really fly, they glide,' added old man Malebranche, 'like this . . .'

He didn't climb up onto the kitchen cupboard to imitate the owl's flight for me, but he spread out his stringy arms which made him look more like a plucked chicken than a bird of the night with a steely beak and murderous talons.

'Have you ever seen anyone go into the other half of my house?' I asked to bring an end to the imitations of winged creatures and to get back to what I was really worrying about, because the ornithological explanations for the terror that I'd experienced left me somewhat dissatisfied.

'Oh, poor boy! No, no one.'

'Not even the Dutchwoman's son?'

She shrugged her shoulders as if to say 'Who knows, where a madman's concerned.'

Then, as if she wanted to put an end to my questions, she said 'But, you will have some *pineau* with us, won't you, Mr . . .'

I thought 'Why not', the way things are at the moment and I replied 'Just a little one, then.'

★

After chain-smoking four cigarettes, I managed to rid myself of the taste of pineau and sugar which could have stayed stuck to my palate for several hours.

Just before reaching my front door, I saw a silhouette up ahead. It was vaguely familiar but I couldn't immediately identify it. It was a man, he had his back to me and I couldn't see his neck which was hunched into his shoulders. He was very small, he was walking slowly and didn't seem to be going anywhere in particular, but he wasn't from La Berthonie, I was quite sure of that. Sensing that there was someone behind him, he turned round and then I recognised the face under the tightly-fitting beret. It was the dead men's father. The lenses of his glasses, thick and yellowing like old mother Malebranche's teeth, concealed any expression that might have been written in his eyes and even his bushy eyebrows seemed to cast a shadow over his eyes. He nodded his head in greeting, without uttering a word. Why was he here? What sort of pilgrimage brought him to this village, a hamlet even, which was so close to his own but in which he was, after all, as good as a foreigner? Was he too looking for some explanation for his sons' deaths in La Berthonie and the surrounding area? Was he wondering why he'd been spared, having lost three of his children, four if you counted his daughter who could no longer stay in the area after the business of the lover whom she herself had denounced to the police? His mother had gone mad. If I went on like that, the list of his misfortunes — all of which were very real, mind you — would have ended up, by their sheer accumulation, seeming comic.

'Would you like to come in and have a drink?'

I felt, as I spoke these words, that my English accent was rather stronger than usual.

'No, thank you.'

He shook his head, looking slightly embarrassed, because he was refusing hospitality from a neighbour and that just wasn't done, even if it wasn't quite so bad in my case because I was English. All the same, he was looking for an excuse. In the end he made do with 'I can't, they're waiting for me. I've got things to do.'

Then, so that I wouldn't feel insulted, he added 'Perhaps next time . . .'

He took advantage of the almost audible suspension points at the end of his sentence to eclipse himself.

It occurred to me that he could be there because he

suspected me. As Martine had said, I was, after all, a foreigner (despite the fact that I'd never come across any evidence of xenophobia in the area), I didn't really work, everyone knows that being a painter is just another way of saying being lazy and my efforts were so few and far between that even I would hesitate to label myself an artist. Not to mention whether or not I had any talent. Then, of course, I lived alone; a fact of which I was only too aware. None of that really gave me a motive, but the accumulation of these characteristics implied a sufficiently dubious character to explain bouts of a sort of murderous madness. Also, if I were guilty, that wouldn't have done anyone any harm, to use a rather unfortunate expression, because the honour of the entire country and certainly of the locals, would have remained intact. The thought that police officers might come and ring at my door (not that I had a doorbell, actually) from one minute to the next left me feeling rather distraught. I'd read sociological studies about overcrowding in prisons and what happened to people like me when they came into contact with real criminals. For now, even if his appalling luck bordered on comedy, I felt pity above all for the silhouette that was trudging away from me, his head whirring with an indescribable nightmare which he alone could understand and which his neighbours contemplated with terror or with a selfish shrug of the shoulders as they thought in their heart of hearts 'Wouldn't want all that bad luck coming down on us'. Then, as everything eventually comes to an end, so did this mood of compassion which, for a moment, had allowed me to believe with some delight in my own profoundly humane feelings.

It was cold in the house. The telephone didn't ring. (Still thinking about Martine. Far better to forget about her, but I was obviously incapable of that and I hated myself for this weakness.) The list of possible walks, all more morbid than each other because they inevitably had some connection with the murders of the last days and weeks, all seemed terrifying but also rather boring, wearying even. It really was incredible how the Dordogne in February could exhaust you with its blood and murder! I was almost, and not without irony, like the murderer who returns to the scene of the crime, an ancient reflex that even psychologists, criminologists and other interested parties found difficult to explain.

It was only the fear that gripped me that revived my interest in the whole subject. Nothing to drink, obviously. I was practically waiting impatiently for night to fall, convinced that the moon and the darkness would bring their own share of terror which might finally break up the nagging monotony of the day. At least the sense of danger made time pass and I'd got to the stage where I was looking out for real reasons — audible, visible, palpable ones — to be afraid.

It was then that I heard the sound of a tractor and I almost envied the Malebranches' son who always had something to do. He must have wondered what it was like to have nothing to do, like me, but he would never be able to imagine it.

Waiting for nightfall had the effect of dragging out time and distance. Sitting in my chair next to the dark fireplace, I thought about, for example, going out and buying something to drink. But it was too far to go and the wind was too cold. I really did have to do something, though. Paint? A landscape? The house? This last suggestion of mine only produced a slightly bitter smile. A nude? No model obviously. Actually . . . no, I preferred not to let my wild imaginings stray any further.

With my hands in my pockets, I wandered round what I called the garden: an expanse of rough grass, dotted with mole-hills, leading down to a huge walnut tree, a typical feature in the area, which formed a tent of foliage in the spring and summer. When I bought the house, I'd thought I would be giving Gertrude Jekyll some stiff competition; the nettles were proof that I would not. Just thinking of her name, that honourable genius of a gardener, made me realise what I really wanted, apart from the perfectly obvious pleasure of opening a bottle of single malt, was a nineteenth- or even eighteenth-century English novel, narrated by a pastor with all sorts of tales of . . . with all sorts of tales of things that happened by a cosy fireside. So I rummaged about in the barn to fetch logs, old newspapers and some vine shoots that old mother Malebranche had sold me at an exorbitant price and which wouldn't have looked out of place thrown over the crooked back of some local or medieval witch. Then I lit the fire. I was so pleased with it that I actually forgot the splendid bucolic and episcopal novel which would have been set in a cottage in the Cotswolds or possibly Yorkshire or Wales, at a push.

*

Eventually, the hour of the white lady struck.

I was sitting in my chair, watching the flames and making a mental inventory of my book collection. Before moving here, I'd bought quantities of interminable Victorian novels, telling myself this was my last chance if I were ever to have any degree of culture and knowledge of the classics. So far I hadn't read a single one, so daunted was I by those dense slabs of paper which I contemplated respectfully on my Ikea shelving unit.

So I was sitting watching the flames, sober, patient, safe and warm, when I heard the scratching sound again. It was difficult at first to recognise it as such. Rather than scratching, it was just an irritating regular sound which emerged above the erratic crackling of the logs and the purring of the flames like the wind blowing off some wild moorland in northern England, an expanse which was now reduced to the dimensions of my stone chimney. Then the quickening heartbeats that I'd been missing all day finally made themselves felt. At last. With more control than on the previous day, because I hadn't had a drop to drink since the *pineau* in the morning. To this day I don't understand the intuition which warned me that I would hear those noises again. Was it my fear which persuaded me to ignore them at first? Then, as if resigning myself to confronting the situation, I pushed myself up out of the chair with a hand on each arm-rest. I stood motionless for a few moments, with my head lowered and my arms hanging by my side, to give myself time to gather my courage. Gather my courage for what? To confront a barn owl? Perhaps. As I looked up, I caught sight of the Trinity Rugby Fifteen. A whole series of clichés reeled off in my mind, I recited three Kipling poems to myself, finishing with *If*, and then I headed for the stairs, crossed the studio and climbed the rope-ladder towards the attic.

When I reached the third rung, my legs started to shake uncontrollably. I remembered old mother Malebranche's imitations and whistlings, but there was nothing in what I could now hear that was remotely like the high-pitched wail that my neighbour's toothless mouth had produced. One of the flat rectangular rungs of the ladder snapped under my weight. And the scratching sound stopped instantly. It was, of course, possible that it was an animal frightened by the noise. I thought of thumping the wall with my foot or of shouting out to see what would happen. But, on the other hand, I wanted to be quite sure that I was dealing with an animal, so I mustn't frighten it away completely. And if it were a white lady making these noises (which hardly seemed likely), I wouldn't be able see her take off, because all the openings in the attic wall were on the other side of the house and I wouldn't hear her either because birds of prey — particularly barn owls — are noted for the total silence in which they swoop onto the unfortunate creatures that they then tear to shreds and devour.

I'd been perfectly still for at least thirty seconds when the noises started up again on the far side of the wall. I went up the remaining steps to the attic, then felt my way forward, with one hand guiding me along the wall, towards the corner opposite the walled-up door. I found an old bit of wood, studded with nails which someone had left there for some inexplicable reason, some inept and useless bit of DIY, a speciality amongst those who live in the country. Armed then with my makeshift club, I crouched in the shadows feeling that this whole business was impossible, that I'd dreamed it, that I was going to wake up at any minute, perhaps I'd even be lying next to Martine while I was at it.

But the scratching sound had given way to a series of sharp knocks. My eyes had become accustomed to the darkness, still not sufficiently, though, for me to see the old cement which held the stones in the door frame beginning to crumble; but I could hear it showering to the floor, like sand poured from a child's bucket. My heart was beating very hard. I was no longer in any doubt. It was a human being at work on the far side, someone trying to prise apart the stones to get into my house, my attic, and it was highly unlikely that his intentions were of a friendly nature. I was going to see him appear before me, the man who killed the three Caminade brothers, who drove their grandmother mad and who was still on the loose in the countryside. My imagination conferred terrifyingly improbable features on him, he was straight out of a children's fairy tale, he would have the face of a gargoyle, a great shock of hair and foam on his lips like the Dutchwoman's mad son. And, as if to confirm my fears, I then heard a rasping breath accompanying each new blow, the laboured breathing of a woodcutter who's beginning to tire but carries on with his task, driven by an intangible, almost supernatural force. I crouched down in the dark. I had no experience or knowledge of violence, except for a few tackles when I was rather shambolically flattened on a rugby pitch, events more closely related to clumsy brutality than to violence. My hand became clammy with sweat as I squeezed the piece of wood with all my strength, not sure that I would know how to use it — if I had the courage or the opportunity to — or whether I would be paralysed with fear, like a rabbit or a rat targeted by the white lady. I could almost envisage this creature that was about to appear spreading out a pair of downy wings like an avenging angel.

A stone broke free and fell to the ground next to me. Then a sort of sigh came to me through the hole it had created. The sigh of a killer who knows that the worst of his job is done and that it's all routine from now on. After a certain point, there are no longer words to express fear, there's just a haze of sounds and images, then silence, perhaps a laugh.

The other stones no longer offered any resistance, they fell one after the other and the assassin, my assassin, no longer made any attempt to work quietly.

Suddenly, as if in a dream, I heard footsteps from his side of the attic rushing towards me as if from very far away, a woman's footsteps coming closer and closer and then a voice, as if another bird were talking to the angel . . . or the barn owl.

'I knew you'd be here, stop it! Stop it, you're drunk.'

A woman's voice, full of energy, quite well-spoken. It seemed impossible and yet how could I not recognise her voice. It was the old Dutchwoman, Rachel.

A man's voice answered her, he had a regional accent, but only very slight, very distant, just the hint of a memory.

'Leave me alone, leave me alone, Rachel, please.'

'You're crazy, stop it.'

'I know what I'm doing. Go on, go away. You're going to ruin everything.'

His voice sounded rather like the doctor's, he too had only a very slight accent. But I was almost sure it wasn't him.

And suddenly, by dint of hearing what amounted to a domestic row going on the far side of this doorway which was re-opening stone by stone — after how many years? — I no longer felt in the least bit afraid, only rather curious. There was also something reassuring about the woman's voice, the voice of a woman old enough to be my mother, a woman who came on the scene like a providential, benevolent apparition to turn the avenging angel away from its evil intentions.

Another stone fell. And I heard Rachel's voice again and the sounds of a struggle.

'Stop it, stop it,' she cried, 'you're hurting me. Let me go.'

I would not have been able, at that moment, to measure the volume of my own voice: did I whisper, did I yell at the top of my lungs? In any event, I pronounced these words: 'Who's there? What are you doing? Go away!'

Everything suddenly stopped. Then a crash. And Rachel's voice saying 'Go away, don't worry about me. Please just go away. And don't worry.'

I heard the man leaving, his heavy, hurried footsteps reverberating on the far-from-sturdy attic floorboards. He went down a staircase. I rushed over to the opening he'd made in the wall. Impossible to see a thing, apart from a vague shape on the floor which I guessed was the old Dutchwoman's body. But I knew about that, I wanted to see the man who'd been with her and who had, quite categorically, wanted to kill me. I hurled myself down my rope-ladder once again. The moon was shining brightly enough to etch murderous shadows on the landscape. I reached the Périgordian balcony and I saw a shaggy, hunched figure lumbering away towards Pisse-Chèvre with the laborious stride of a prop forward. I didn't recognise him straight away because none of what had happened would have made me think of him, because I hadn't seen him very often and then there was his accent, his trace of a regional accent, but the man that I saw running away, the man who'd wanted to kill me, I was quite sure of it, even though I still didn't have any proof, this man who now seemed so pitiful, was the Englishman from Pisse-Chèvre.

At that moment, I sensed a presence quite close to me, it was the false old Dutchwoman coming back out of the house.

'Hey, *madame*! Wait!'

I was afraid of only one thing and it seemed paltry compared to what I had just been through: that she too would take to her heels, leaving me there, still alive but still completely ignorant of the whole business with which she must surely be familiar. I saw her look to the left and then the right, not understanding where my voice was coming from.

'Up here,' I said, 'I'm on the balcony.'

She looked up and smiled at me. This all seemed completely incongruous, but at least a sense of calm had been re-established, if not any semblance of reality. It does have to be said that in February, in the Dordogne, you end up getting everything muddled up.

'Please, please don't go,' I begged her. 'I'd like to talk to you.'

She stayed where she was. She didn't look as if she particularly wanted to run away, but she didn't reply either.

'Don't move, don't move, I'm coming down,' I said, waving my arms as if I were afraid of missing a meeting that would have a great impact on my future, which wasn't far from the truth.

*

'Come in, sit down.'

'Thank you.'

She was grey with dust all down one side of her face and her dress. He'd probably pushed her and she'd fallen on the attic floor where I'd seen her or vaguely made her out earlier, through the hole in the walled-up doorway.

'Would you like something to drink, I haven't much to . . .'

'A glass of water, please, I'm very thirsty.'

She spoke without meeting my eye, like a criminal at the police station talking to the arresting officer.

I should have been furious with her. After all, I was convinced that someone had tried to do away with me that very evening and that the assassin was known to her, judging by the familiar tone with which she'd addressed the person concerned and the content of her conversation with him. And yet I felt something for her, a sort of . . . no, it wasn't pity, or compassion. She knew everything and I knew nothing. I was waiting for her to be so good as to give me some explanations. Liking, I felt a liking for her. Especially as she had possibly just saved my life. My fear had reached such a pitch of intensity a few minutes earlier that it completely altered all my reactions, as if I were interpreting the events and acting on them under the effects of some kind of anaesthesia, which might have come across as courage.

'Thank you,' she said as I handed her the glass of water.

'Don't mention it. Are you sure you won't have anything else? I . . .'

'No, no, I'm fine.'

She sat with one elbow resting on the table and her head lowered. Her slender wrinkled hands, bearing a sumptuous engagement ring and a wedding ring in old gold, were clamped round the glass as she brought it to her lips. She drank half of it, put it back down and then ran her hands over the wooden table top as if she were smoothing a table cloth or preparing to read the future in a pack of cards. While I waited, I sat down at the table opposite her.

She looked up at me with her blue-grey eyes and contemplated me with an almost maternal expression. There was a vague plea for forgiveness in those eyes, probably because someone had just tried to kill me and everything that had happened had probably been most unpleasant for me, she could see that. (I was obsessed with the idea that someone had wanted to strangle me or to sink a knife into my heart or to use goodness knows what other method. Anyway, I don't like to think about it in too much detail, but anyone finding themselves in a simi-lar situation would quickly realise that you don't tend to get over it that quickly.)

'You've worked it out,' she said with a rather sad smile.

13

'Not altogether, to be honest.'

'Really?'

'Was that the Englishman from Pisse-Chèvre that I just saw on the track?'

'Did you see him?'

'Yes.'

'The Englishman from Pisse-Chèvre . . . as you say. He's no more English than you or I.'

It was tempted to tell her that she might be a Dutchwoman who wasn't actually Dutch and the Englishman from Pisse-Chèvre might be no more English than she was or no more Dutch than I was, but for my part, I was indeed born in England, there was absolutely no doubt about that and my parents were by way of being respectable people. But I didn't actually say anything.

It was she who realised what she'd just said and, almost laughing, she added 'No more English than I am, anyway. And I'm not even Dutch, as you already know. Poor Jacky . . .'

'Sorry?'

'My poor Jacques . . .'

'You mean the owner of the other half of the house?'

'Yes, Jacques, my Jacky. You see, the Englishman from Pisse-Chèvre is only really Jacky.'

'Your lover?'

I immediately regretted this interjection, but it was too late.

She raised her eyebrows.

'You certainly seem to know a lot for someone who still hasn't worked it all out.'

She seemed more amused than annoyed.

'Yes, my lover, as you said,' she went on. 'Oh well, at least people talk to each other round here.'

'I'm so sorry.'

'Oh, don't be. It's the truth anyway.'

'That's why he got into the house so easily.'

She looked at me as if I were at last showing signs that my cranial cavity accommodated a brain.

'Yes, that's why. He had the keys. You see, it was easy.'

'But was he coming to kill me this evening?' I asked with a note of fear in my voice.

'Yes, poor Jacky . . .'

That left me quite speechless. A man, an impostor, had come to disembowel me in my own home and there she was talking about him in that pitying, tearful voice.

'Poor Jacky! Poor Jacky! And what about me?'

'It's quite a long story, you know.'

'It was very nearly cut short for me.'

'You've got a good grasp of the language, haven't you?'

'That's not really the point,' I replied rather curtly before asking 'And did he kill the others too?'

'Yes, you see, he's got more reason to be pitied than you. So have I, actually,' she said with a shrug of her shoulders.

My anger subsided. She was right.

'And what's going to happen now?'

It occurred to me that she might have been this man's accomplice, since she had been his mistress. And yet she'd saved my life. What I had trouble understanding was why there had been any need to kill me.

'Because he felt that you were spying on him. He thought you'd worked it all out, you see, he knew you'd been to see the doctor. Ever since you witnessed that scene on the day of the funeral vigil, when he was drunk and his daughter was watching him.'

'Did you see me?'

'Of course. Just as I saw that you followed me to Pisse-Chèvre the other day.'

I felt myself blush. At the same time I noticed that my embarrassment seemed to please her, a meagre revenge for the lack of discretion I'd displayed, because at the end of the day I'd never had a valid reason for carrying out an investigation of any sort.

'Anyway,' she said, 'if you're going to understand, I'll have to start at the beginning. And that was a very long time ago . . . that sounds like a fairy tale,' she commented a little bitterly. 'It was during the war. Because Jacky and I are the same age, you see.

'This was the unoccupied zone here, my father was a Jew from Alsace and I was about ten when we arrived. But when the Germans breached the demarcation line, we had to go into hiding. Well, my mother, my sisters and I did, because for that whole period my father was tortured — mentally, I mean — by his own conscience. He didn't know what he should do and he ended up joining one of the Resistance groups, the same group that had found us a hiding place.'

'Marcel's network?'

'Sorry?' she said with a jump, as if suddenly remembering that I was there. As if I'd interrupted a monologue at the wrong moment.

'Um . . . Marcel, I mean . . .'

'Ah, so you know Marcel?' she said with a slight smile. 'He set his cap at me after the war, our dear Marcel. He was a little older than me, he must have been in his twenties when I was seventeen, something like that, well, it doesn't make much difference . . . At the time I was in love with Jacky, but that was after the war, we haven't got to that yet. So we were hiding on a farm, in a barn, because the old farmer's wife was too frightened to have us in the house. And that was understandable. She hid all of us. That's where I met Jacky. We were just two children and we played together, nothing very exciting about that, but then our fathers ended up in the same Resistance network and we never knew when we might be given bad news, which in my case would have been doubly bad because I could have been arrested and deported, even if at the time, at my age then, I didn't really realise it. We never stayed in one place for long, we had to keep moving. But you know about that, everyone knows that now . . . or nearly. Then one day, someone informed on us, us and the whole Resistance group that my father and Jacky's father and Marcel belonged to. They were ambushed and my father was killed. But when the Germans came for us . . .'

'The business with the stinging nettles?'

She raised her eyebrows once again.

'Well, I must say, you've done your research. I didn't know people were still talking about it.'

'Marcel told me.'

'Him again. What I'm sure he didn't tell you was that the person who informed on us all didn't know that their own son was in the group and was captured in the ambush. He was tortured in Périgueux and then he died in a concentration camp.'

'Yes. He did tell me that.'

'Well, then, you know who it was, you know who gave us all away?'

'No. Marcel told me that it was a woman and that she was killed by the Resistance soon afterwards.'

'He was saying what he wished had happened rather than the truth, not for the first time. Dear Marcel. No, she wasn't killed and she lived very comfortably. Of course she wasn't. It's the old woman. She gave us all away. Old grand-mother Caminade who's gone mad now and well she deserves it.'

'So the ghost, the devil talking in patois, was that . . .'

'Yes, but wait, we're not there yet. After the war, at the time of the Liberation, she told everyone that it was Jacky's mother — who'd lost her husband — who'd done it. Her head was shaved and she was publicly humiliated. And the old bitch, who wasn't so old at the time, watched her evil work with satisfaction, as if she were avenging her son's death — which she herself had brought about. And of course Jacky, who was a teenager at the time, had to watch the whole thing. His mother committed suicide soon after that. She hanged herself.'

'And what about the other members of the Resistance group, like Marcel? Couldn't they do anything about it, couldn't they say that Jacky's mother was innocent?'

'They weren't there. Marcel had joined the regular army and was heading for Strasbourg when all this was going on. And people weren't asking too many questions. You wouldn't understand. Likewise, you won't understand that the same old mother Caminade pretty much adopted Jacky, that he lived at the farmhouse with them and the oddest thing about it is that they didn't treat him any worse than any of the others, when you might have thought they'd treat him like a slave or a whipping boy. But no, you see . . . the Caminades made use of the situation to rob him of his inheritance, I don't know how they did it, I don't understand legal things. Be that as it may, when he came back from his mother's burial, Jacky was told that all he'd been left was half a house.'

'What about his sisters? He had sisters.'

'He didn't get on with them. They were older than him and they got married and scarpered as soon as they could to get away from this whole business. As you know, Jacky and I were alone, we grew up together and we became lovers. For a while. And then . . .'

'You married the Dutchman.'

'Exactly,' she replied, tilting her chin up defiantly. 'I'm not going to go into all the details, I was only young, I was lonely, I was very frightened, etc. Then, some time later, the English officer who'd commanded the Resistance group came back to visit the area with his parents. He heard what had happened to Jacky, and his father — the officer's father — offered to take Jacky back to England, out of compassion or as an act of charity, I don't know. You know that the English are given to rather ostentatious acts of charity,' she said with a hint of contempt which, in the circumstances, struck me as unfair even if, on the whole, she wasn't altogether wrong.

'He was in his early twenties and, at first, he only got jobs as a servant or a cleaner, that sort of thing. Then pretty soon, he did rather well out of it, he learned to speak English, obviously, but he never really lost the last trace of his French accent. That's why, when he did come back to live here, he didn't mix with the English and he always pretended to be deaf. But it's not true. It was so that he didn't have to talk to anyone. He was turning into the Englishman from Pisse-Chèvre.'

'Jacky . . .' she whispered after a brief silence filled with all her painful memories, with all the years and with all the affection that she still felt for him, as if he were a reflection of herself, uncontrollable, murderous and justifiably angry. And all these thoughts culminated in that name which she uttered like a sigh.

I didn't say anything and she understood that my silence was an invitation to her to continue.

'Well, eventually, the old Englishman who'd more or less adopted Jacky died, leaving him a relatively large sum of money.

They were rich, you see . . . well-to-do. The young English officer had got married and moved to London after qualifying as a lawyer or something like that. Meanwhile, Jacky had become friends . . . more than friends with the piano teacher who taught the old Englishman's grandchildren. She had a rather suspect past, even Jacky who's lived with her for long enough, has never found out all of it. Well, that's what he said, anyway. On top of that, this woman had a daughter by someone else, history doesn't relate who he was. It's the woman you saw, a secretive sort of creature . . . but then as time passes and with everything that's been going on, we've all become secretive . . . well . . . Now, where was I?'

'Isn't she Jacky's daughter then?'

'No, no. The piano teacher was another black sheep that this Englishman took under his wing. I've always thought that he must have been paying for something he'd done . . . I don't know why. Anyway, that's another story. This one's already complicated enough as it is. And no question of saying anything like that to Jacky, he'd be furious. Either way, a few years after his benefactor's death, he decided to come back here. Like an assassin returning to the scene of a crime he hasn't yet committed. Or, in Jacky's case, like a ghost coming back to haunt his torturers. But I don't think he really had that in mind when he came back. No one will ever know exactly what was going on in his head at the time. He was like one of those animals that returns to its birthplace. I don't know . . . even I don't know.'

'He still owned half of this house. He paid his taxes and everything.'

'Yes, that's odd, isn't it? He never managed to sever the ties with this house. And, to be honest, he wanted the Caminades to know that he was still alive and this half-house was like an image of their guilt because it still belonged to their victim. And that's also why he didn't come back here to the house. He bought

Isidore's house in Pisse-Chèvre and passed himself off as an Englishman. He was just five minutes' walk from the people he hated most in the world, with a loathing that amounted to madness. The piano teacher and her daughter followed him here.'

'And what about the phone number on the outskirts of Paris, which they rang and rang, but where no one ever answered?'

She shrugged, paused for a moment and then burst out laughing.

'Yes, there was that business, too. In fact, it had nothing to do with him. Obviously there's more than one Jacques Duroc in France. They were all going crazy ringing this number so that they could get their hands on this half-house and there was never any reply. I'm sure you can imagine how they puzzled over it. And because there was no reply, they were convinced that it was the right number, Jacky's number. Extraordinary logic, isn't it?'

I was careful not to tell her that I'd reached exactly the same conclusion for exactly the same reason.

'I wouldn't mind another glass of water,' she said after a moment.

When I came back from the kitchen — with my hands shaking so much they splattered droplets of water all over the floor — she went on with her story.

'I think the two women, his wife and his daughter, as people call her, didn't really have any choice. It's rather strange. The daughter was only a child at the time but I've sometimes suspected that Jacky knew something about her mother and he used this knowledge to force her to come here with him. Well . . . what does it matter . . . anyway, now . . .'

'But how did he end up killing people?'

'He should never have come back here, but it was stronger than him. Then he started drinking, I think that when he came back he thought he was now somehow free to go mad, if you see what I mean. He hung about in the woods, he saw the Caminades all the time, he'd watch them, he hated them. Except for father Caminade. Perhaps the old man had protected him once, I don't know. Perhaps there wasn't any particular reason. But one day, it was the eighth of May, I'm sure you'll understand why . . .'

'Um, no.'

'The end of the war,' she explained in a baffled voice.

'Oh yes, sorry, forgive me.'

'On the eighth of May, then, he saw the old woman.'

'The one who'd given them all away?'

'Yes. She was with her whole family and they were laying a spray of flowers on the war memorial.'

Even she couldn't help herself smiling with obvious disgust when she remembered this demonstration of outrageous cheek.

'And one of the sons went into the bar straight afterwards. Jacky watched the whole thing, that might have been the straw that broke the camel's back. Especially as he'd been drinking far too much ever since he'd moved into Pisse-Chèvre. It's funny . . . I'm already talking about him in the past tense . . . As if Jacky were already dead. He's died so many times . . . so anyway, he gave the boy a lift in his car. They went and had a drink together and when the boy was completely drunk, because of course he couldn't hold his drink so well, Jacky knocked him out and went and drowned him in the lake near Nontron. I don't know why his family let him go with Jacky, they all thought he was a deaf, drunken Englishman. I do know one thing, though, which might explain why: there was another boy with Jacky that day, my son.'

She stopped to give me time to take this information on board. That was the murder that he'd witnessed as a teenager and from which he would never recover. When he came to my door saying. 'He's dead, isn't he, he's dead', he was talking about this body swollen with water. Then, as the silence continued, I realised that she was hesitating before entrusting another secret to me, because these kinds of secrets are inevitably all interlinked and end up forming a coherent architecture in which each stone, each lie, each crime has its own importance.

'Because your son . . .' I began, without daring to finish the sentence.

'Yes, he's Jacky's son.'

Then she tilted her head right back and something close to relief appeared on her face.

'He doesn't even know himself, that Jacky's his father.'

'How old is he?'

'Madmen are sort of ageless, aren't they?' she said, on the defensive, as if I'd insulted her personally by asking this question. Then in a more conciliatory tone, she replied 'He's thirty. Why do you ask?'

'I don't really know.'

'Do you want to know the rest?'

I wasn't quite sure at that point. But she didn't wait for a reply before going on.

'That was all fifteen years ago. But recently the crimes have picked up speed. The one before last, which was the second, was disguised as an accident. Then there was the last one, a stabbing committed in front of the old woman, as you now know. After the first crime, I panicked. But my priority was to look after my son, even though at the same time I was praying that Jacky wouldn't be taken from me. Afterwards, I probably should have called the police, alerted the doctor, I don't know. I didn't. I kept begging Jacky, I was trying to . . . I don't know. That's why you found me in tears at his house at Pisse-Chèvre the other day, I knew he'd killed another one. Another of the old woman's grandsons who had nothing to do with . . . with all this.'

'What are you going to do?'

'I don't know.'

'He's killing innocent people.'

She looked at me a tad impatiently and it's true I could have done without uttering that banality and the one that followed: 'And he's dangerous.'

She quite evidently didn't need me to tell her that and for a moment I wondered whether she'd made these confessions to me so that I could act for her.

'And this evening, was he coming to kill me?'

'Obviously.'

'Why me?' I asked, almost protesting.

If he kills his neighbours, fine, but I thought that having a shot at me was taking things a little too far.

'I've already told you. He'd noticed that you were following me, I'd told him about you and told him to be careful, that he was drawing attention to himself and that there was an Englishman, a real one, nearby. That he was taking too many risks. Then the daughter saw you go to the doctor and everyone realised that . . . you were leading the investigation,' she concluded with an ironic smile.

I swallowed with difficulty.

'And you, now? What are you going to do?' she asked me.

It wasn't a bad question. It struck me as virtually impossible not to get involved in this whole business which had nothing to do with me, as I had been from the start. And it would be equally impossible for me to do my share of informing. But surely I couldn't let a madman carry on running riot in the countryside, killing people aged between thirty and forty to get his revenge on an old woman, who was still alive to boot, for what she'd done to him nearly sixty years earlier? And what about the piano teacher who'd made me think of Grantchester? And her daughter? And what about me, who had so nearly succumbed to the blows of the false Englishman from Pisse-Chèvre and the real Jacky?

'You see,' she said. 'You know as well as I do that something's got to be done, but you don't know how to go about it.'

14

It was Jacky himself who gave us the answer. And even that, in the light of the life he'd led, was an injustice. He committed suicide that same night with a shotgun. He put both barrels under his chin and squeezed the trigger with the help of a little stick. There was nothing left of his face. The two women who lived with him were woken by the sound of the shot. There was no telephone at Pisse-Chèvre, so they ran over to the Malebranches who called the ambulance.

This time I was the one who thought 'poor Jacky'.

I didn't see Rachel, the old Dutchwoman again. We were probably the only two people to know what had really happened. Unless everyone in the area actually knew after all. It didn't matter now. I'd promised myself that I wouldn't talk about it to the Malebranches, but they brought the subject up by mentioning the terrible accident that had taken the life of my compatriot. I'm sure they didn't believe a word of it.

The two Englishwomen contacted the young officer's son. He came and dealt with everything. He arranged — and this is not without a certain irony — to have Jacky's body repatriated to England, so that he could be buried there, over the Channel. Pisse-Chèvre, Isidore's old house, is for sale.

Mine's already sold. The buyers were told, without going into too much detail, that it would be possible to buy both halves of the house.

I often think back to the month of February in the

Dordogne, but I never talk about it. I now live in a two-room studio in Islington, I'm surrounded by crime, but you can't see it and you can't hear it, you just have to avoid thinking about it.